Blood Trail

Blood
Trail

NANCY SPRINGER

Holiday House / New York

Library of Congress Cataloging-in-Publication Data
Springer, Nancy.
Blood trail / Nancy Springer.— 1st ed.
p. cm.
Summary: After his best friend is murdered, seventeen-year-old Booger
realizes he is the only one who has any idea who might have committed
the crime—but he doesn't dare tell anyone.
ISBN 0-8234-1723-9 (hardcover)
[1. Murder—Fiction. 2. Grief—Fiction. 3. Mystery and detective
stories.] I. Title.

PZ7.S76846 Bl 2003
[Fic]—dc21   2002027628

To Jaime

chapter one

"Crawdad fight!" Aaron yelled, holding a humongous crayfish in one hand as he lunged through the water at me. He aimed its claws toward my face. "C'mon, Jeremy, defend yourself!"

I yipped and dived for the bottom of the river, searching for a weapon of my own. All I saw were itty-bitty crayfish sending up puffs of silt as they backed under rocks. How had Aaron caught that monster? It was practically the size of a lobster, and pissed off. If it got its claws on my bare skin, it would give me one hell of a nip. Trust Aaron to grab the biggest, baddest crawdad in the swimming hole—

And here he came, diving at me in a rush of bubbles, that hellacious crawdad aimed my way. Even underwater, he was grinning.

Crawdad fight, my eye. I didn't stand a chance. I pushed off the bottom of the swimming hole and shot to the surface, where I sucked in a big breath of air. Then I swam hard toward shore.

There was an Aaron-size splash behind me as he sur-faced. "Booger," he yelled, "where you going?" He sounded puppy-dog hurt, but I knew he was clowning around. I mean, Aaron and I had been friends since third grade. When we were little, he used to fool me, but now we were starting senior year, and I knew when he was kidding.

"You think you're hot snot on a silver platter," he yelled, "but you're just a cold Booger on a paper plate!"

I started laughing, which is not a good idea when you're trying to swim. Water went up my nose and made me cough. Aaron swam after me, but he was splashing like a hippo, because with that crayfish in one hand he couldn't swim right. Even coughing, I got to the boulders at the edge of the river in plenty of time to haul myself out and look around for some kind of counter-crawdad armament. Okay, my bike helmet. Aaron and I had been biking to get in shape for foot-ball, and we'd stopped at the river for a swim.

He did an end around past the boulders and climbed out of the river, still grinning, still wielding his giant crayfish. "Better give it up, Booger," he teased.

"No way, nimrod." Arms outstretched, bike helmet in both hands as a shield, I faced off with him.

"Then prepare to be creamed." Aaron advanced with crayfish at the ready.

With every step he took the crawdad looked bigger. "Jeez, man," I said, "that thing's enormous. You should take it home and feed your family."

2

Just like that, Aaron's hand dropped, and he lost his grin. He turned away from me, crouched by the river, and let the crayfish go scuttling back into the water. Without a word he sat on a boulder, just staring.

What the hey? I had no idea. I parked myself on another boulder and did some staring myself, watching the minnows swarming in the sunlit shallows at the river's edge. My wet shorts trickled on the rock. The sun dried my shoulders.

After a while I asked, "What's the matter?"

Aaron muttered, "Nothing."

"C'mon, Aaron. What's got you torqued?"

He sighed, then said, "Family, schmamily. I don't want to go home."

"How come?"

There could have been lots of reasons, like too many decisions waiting for him, whether to join the army or go to college, all that. Or maybe he was in trouble with his parents because his kid sister had ratted on him about something. Or maybe he was fighting with his brother. Or maybe his parents were fighting with each other. I expected him to say something like that.

But what he actually said was, "Booger, I'm scared."

I was so surprised, I didn't say anything. Just for a minute I thought he was setting up one of his jokes, like the time he got into the girls' locker room and switched all the bras around.

"I mean it, Jeremy!" He wasn't clowning. He faced me with his eyes shadowy dark, with his round face stark serious. "I'm scared."

"Huh?" I didn't have a clue what he was talking about.

He said, "Huh, hell, pay attention," but he didn't roll his eyes as usual.

I said, "Scared to go home? You mean, like, today?"

"Noooo, next year. Duh." But he didn't smile. He looked down, picked up a round stone, and held it like an egg in his hand.

"How come?"

"Just—I've got this stupid feeling. Like something's gonna happen."

In all the years I'd known Aaron, I'd hardly ever seen him without a big grin spreading across his chipmunk cheeks. I mean, we could be two yards from our own goal line and Aaron would still grin. But not now.

I said, "Something's going to happen? Like what?"

Aaron stared at the river. He tossed the stone into the water, splat. The minnows scattered.

"Nothing," he muttered.

We were back where we'd started. "Nothing, my ass. What's the matter? What are you scared of?"

He pressed his lips together, but then he said it. "Nathan."

His brother.

4

"Nathan? What about him?" I'd barely seen Nathan all summer. Maybe if Aaron and I were at his house watching a movie, Nathan might ghost through. Never said anything. Mostly he just stayed in his room with the shades pulled down. But Nathan was always weird that way, at least for the past couple of years, anyway.

I asked, "You guys been fighting?" Once, back in eighth grade, they fought so bad, Aaron broke Nathan's arm.

It was hard to believe Aaron and Nathan were twins—not identical twins, just the other kind. They were both a lot of fun—at least Nathan used to be fun—but they were way different. Aaron was like a big friendly golden retriever, always wanting to play catch or go for a walk, whatever. Everybody liked him. But Nathan was more like one of those racing dogs, a grey-hound, all edges, always in a hurry to get somewhere. When he grinned, it was more like he was showing his teeth. Nathan was a cut master. Some kids kind of admired him, but not like friends. More like spectators. Nobody hassled Nathan, because he could carve you up just by saying something. A guy's got to be good at verbal abuse in high school, and Nathan was the best. Not just abuse, but any kind of talk. Nathan was a brain. He was on the debate team, and teachers said he was brilliant, but for some reason he didn't do great in school. Aaron got better grades—I could never figure why.

I said, "What's wrong with Nathan?"

"Oh, nothing." Aaron got up, flexing his muscles,

and reached for his shirt. "Come on, I gotta get back. Ma said I have to unload the dishwasher and stuff."

"Aaron—"

"Come on, Booger. I'm just being stupid. Imagining things."

Whatever it was, I figured he would tell me about it when he was ready.

We pushed the bikes up a shale slope, then pedaled along the river road. Aaron pumped his dirt bike like he had a devil after him. It was all curves, all uphill, with scrub pine and locust trees leaning over us tired and gray at the end of summer, with the bored old Appalachian Mountains looking down. Aaron rode so hard he kept me out of breath all the way back to the development.

A brick sign at the entrance said PEERAGE HEIGHTS, which is really stretching it in an armpit town like Pinto River. I mean, it's just a half-dead coal town along a rocky, polluted river with a goofy name, Pinto, nobody knows why, and there's nothing classy about living here. Peerage Heights? We're sure not nobility and there isn't any hill. Why don't they ever give developments names like Possum Swamp or Roadkill Hollow? But they don't. It's Peerage Heights. Aaron and I rode on back to our street, Regency Drive.

We got to my house first and stopped the bikes at the bottom of the driveway. By then I was thinking about a drink of water and my aching legs and not much else. "Well, see you at practice," I said.

But Aaron had that weird look on his face again. "Jeremy, do me a favor? Call me in about ten minutes."

"Huh?" I was fumbling to get my stupid bike helmet off my sweaty head. I hate bike helmets, but Coach had made us promise to wear them.

Aaron didn't even say *Huh, hell, pay attention.* He just stared at me, shadowy-eyed.

Hands under my chin, I stared back at him. "Call you? Why?"

"No reason. Just call me." Aaron made it like an order, then got out of there fast so I wouldn't ask anything more.

Aaron was a big guy, and his bike looked too small for him as he rode away. He had his helmet off already, hanging by its straps from his arm. The sun on his buzz-cut hair made it look kind of reddish.

I got my helmet off, feeling dead tired. Worn out. I stomped into my house and glubbed water in the kitchen, just wanting a few minutes of peace—but nah, in the next room my kid sister, Jamy, was parked in front of the TV with three of her pimply middle-school girlfriends. The three extra brats squealed like guinea pigs when they saw me.

"Oooh, it's Jeremy!"

"Stud muffin!" That was Aaron's kid sister, Aardy. Well, her real name was Cecily, but everybody called her Aardy, because Aaron said she looked like an aardvark.

"Look at those big sweaty muscles!"

at those big sweaty feet!"

at that big sweaty booger nose!"

Cecily, "You should talk, aardvark nose." Actually, she just had a narrow face, like her brother Nathan—half brother, I mean. Mrs. Gingrich had been married before. But Mr. Gingrich always acted like he was really Nathan and Aaron's father.

"Your nose is uglier!" Aardy yelled.

"But *studly,*" cooed one of the other brats.

"Okay, studly ugly."

"I want to marry you, Jeremy!"

"Sure. Tomorrow," I grumped, heading past them and giving Jamy a whack on the head because she was laughing. She yelled "Ow!" and laughed harder. Once I got to my room and slammed the door, I flopped on my bed. It was more than ten minutes, more like fifteen, before I got up to go look for a snack and remembered I was supposed to call Aaron.

"Ooooh, your brother smells so *good!*" Aardy squealed at Jamy as I barged through on my way to the kitchen phone.

"Shut up," I said. They laughed. Trying to tune them out, I hit the quick-dial for Aaron's number.

His phone rang three times, then somebody picked it up and put it down again without saying a word.

"Huh." I hung up, then picked up again and hit redial. The phone rang four times, then the answering

8

machine at Aaron's place said, "You have reached the Gingrich residence . . . ."

"Damn it!" I waited for the beep, then said, "Aaron, it's Jeremy. Pick up, would you?"

Nothing.

"Aaron?"

Nothing.

"Aaron, pick up!"

Nothing, except the TV room got quiet and Jamy called, "Jeremy, what's wrong?"

Okay, I was freaked out, and she'd heard it in my voice. I slammed down the phone.

"Jamy, listen, I gotta go home," Aardy said all of a sudden. Sounded like her chest was tight, like she was about to have one of her asthma attacks. Not that I really noticed. I was pacing around the kitchen, breathing deep before I tried Aaron's number again. Three rings . . .

"Hello." Somebody had picked up. I felt a wash of relief.

"Hi, Nathan?" It was Nathan; I knew his voice, flat and edgy, like a rectangle. "Is Aaron there?" Stupid question—I knew he was.

"No," Nathan said.

"He isn't?" Forget relief. I started to get that freaky feeling again. "Where'd he go?"

"He's not home." Nathan hung up.

I just stood there a minute before I turned to see Jamy in the kitchen doorway staring at me. "Jeremy, what's going on?"

"Bye, Jamy!" sang the other two girls as they left after Aardy. They'd smelled trouble and bailed. Good move.

I told Jamy, "Listen, tell Mom I went to Aaron's." I headed out the garage door. Saw Aardy running toward her house, her ponytail flapping. She shouldn't be running if her asthma was bothering her.

"Hey, bung brain, you're supposed to be cleaning the basement!" Jamy yelled after me.

I met Mom coming in the driveway, and she told me the same thing—well, she didn't call me bung brain, but she told me no, I wasn't going anywhere, get back in the house and get the trash out of the cellar, it was a firetrap.

Mom and Dad are divorced, and I get stuck with most of the grunt work because he doesn't come around. Which is not really his fault, because Mom can't seem to forgive him and she gives him freezing hell if he comes near her. So all his jobs got passed on to me, including the basement.

I was pissed. I kept telling Mom I had to go to Aaron's right away and she kept asking why and I didn't have an answer. I mean, what could I tell her?

So about five minutes later, I was down in the household dungeon by the washer and dryer, piling empty Tide boxes into a garbage bag and swearing to myself, when a siren went screaming past my house.

That sound went through me like a jolt from a stun gun. I mean, it's not exactly commonplace where we live. The road doesn't go anywhere except around the development. "Mom!" I yelled, running upstairs. "What was that, where did it—"

She and Jamy were both standing in the front door-way looking out. Toward Aaron's house. "Ambulance," Mom said as another siren blared and a police car swept past.

I started sweating like a spaghetti pot. "Mom, I've *got* to get to Aaron's house. Please."

She and Jamy both turned at the same time and gave me the same long look. Finally Mom asked one more time, "Why?"

I blurted out part of it. "He said he was scared, Mom!"

Jamy said, "He kept trying to call him on the phone—"

I yelled at her, "Shut up!"

Mom said, "Jeremy," in a warning voice, and asked Jamy, "Aaron phoned here?"

"No. Butthead kept trying to phone Aaron."

Mom didn't even frown at her for calling me Butthead, just looked at me. "You think something happened to him?"

"I don't *know*!"

"Stop shouting, Jeremy. Calm down. We'll go see what's happening as soon as you calm down."

11

chapter two

Calm. I had to stay calm.

We took the car to get there faster. The minute Mom drove around the curve in the road, I could see that yeah, it really was Aaron's house. Ambulance going blinky-blink in the driveway, two police cruisers with their lights going in front, crowd of neighbors on the lawn with a cop motioning at them to get back, guy in an orange vest waving at us to drive past.

Mom stopped anyway and yelled at him, "What happened?"

"I don't know, lady. You can't stop there. Keep moving."

"Let me out, Mom," I said.

"Me, too!" Jamy butted in from the backseat.

Mom drove on without answering either of us and pulled over in the first place she could find. Before she could stop me, I jumped out and ran back toward Aaron's house.

A state police car screamed in as I ran. The crowd

swarmed all over the lawn and the edge of the road now, most of them people from the development. I saw one of my mom's friends with her hand on her mouth like she might puke, her eyes spooky wide. I saw the old guy who mowed lawns looking grim like a soldier. I saw little kids not playing, just huddled together like it was cold. I saw a couple of fire department guys trying to help the cops push people back. What scared me the most—

Calm. Stay calm.

The worst thing was the way the cops looked as panicky as I was trying not to feel. Cops shouldn't look that way.

"What happened?" I asked the first person I came to, a neighbor lady. She just stared with the funniest look, like she was made of wood, like she couldn't hear me. I pushed past her into the crowd, still hoping—I don't know what I was hoping. That it wasn't Aaron, I guess. That some old guy had snuck into his house to throw a heart attack or something.

"What happened?" I asked again.

A few heads turned, but nobody answered. For a big crowd, it was so quiet it was weird. All I heard was somebody crying somewhere behind me, and off to the side some guy saying, "The little kids shouldn't see. They ought to get them out of here."

I saw the state trooper come out of the house with his face fish-belly pale.

I grabbed the old lawn-mower guy by the arm. "What *happened*?"

He turned and glared at me, but he said, "Kid's dead. Stabbed to death."

"*What?* What kid?" My heart was pounding so hard it hurt.

The old guy turned away without answering, but I already knew the answer.

No. It couldn't be. It had to be some other kid. For some reason, somebody had stabbed Aardy, or Nathan—

But no, I could see Nathan standing in the doorway with his sister hanging onto him sideways, her face hidden behind his back. He acted like he barely knew she was there. His arms hung straight down at his sides. Even at that distance, I could see how white his narrow face was. And I could see dark stains on his T-shirt, like he'd been painting or something.

But it couldn't be Aaron who was dead. It had to be somebody else. Some neighbor kid. *Please.*

Heads turned as a Volvo swerved into the driveway and stopped. Aaron's dad got out and ran toward the house, still in his grocer's apron, with his sleeves rolled up. He must have been at the store when he got the call. The state trooper met him in front of the door.

The crowd was so quiet, I could hear almost every word.

". . . according to your daughter, Cecily, the body is that of your stepson Aaron. I'm sorry, sir."

14

"He's *dead*?" Mr. Gingrich's voice cracked like glass.

Aardy must not have realized her dad was there until she heard his voice. Then she let go of Nathan and darted out the door to her father. One glimpse of her face, and I had to close my eyes.

"Yes, sir, he is dead," said the police officer. "I'm sorry—"

"No. That can't be." Mr. Gingrich's voice. I looked, and saw him patting Aardy's shoulders as she hugged the rough cloth of his apron, but he barely seemed to know what he was doing. "Nathan—" Mr. Gingrich reached toward Nathan, who was standing a few feet away from him inside the front door. But Nathan didn't look like he'd heard.

The trooper edged over to stand between Mr. Gingrich and the door. "If you'll wait in the cruiser—"

Mr. Gingrich shook his head. "There's some kind of mistake." Pulling away from Aardy, he tried to head into the house. "Let me see him. Let me see."

I heard Aardy sobbing. I couldn't look at her.

"We advise against it, sir. We will ask you to identify his clothing—"

"Let me see my son!"

Someone pulled at my elbow. I turned. It was Mom. She didn't say anything, just motioned with her head for me to follow her, and I did. I couldn't handle watching Mr. Gingrich anymore.

15

A couple of cops were stretching yellow plastic ribbon between the crowd and the house, edging people back, back. Mom led me out of there. At the edge of the crowd, Jamy stood hugging herself and shaking. Her voice shook, too, as she said, "Mom, Aardy's crying."

"I know."

"I saw one of the cops puking into a paper bag."

"Hush."

"I heard—"

"Jamy, hush. Good grief . . ." Mom stared past me. I turned and saw a TV news van pulling in at the Gingriches' place.

Mom said, "Come on before it gets even worse." She herded both of us back toward the car.

But when we got there, she didn't get in. She made Jamy get in, but she stopped me, and her eyes had that look like when my dad left.

Very softly she asked, "Jeremy, how did you know?"

I didn't feel like I knew anything, and all of a sudden I wanted to cry. I could barely talk. "Mom, not now."

"Yes, now!" Then her tone changed. "Honey, tell me. Please. You know we have to call the police. Are you going to need a lawyer?"

I shook my head. Damn, I wasn't going to cry. I made my voice hard. "Just call them. Never mind. I'll tell them myself. I'm going back." I turned away.

"Jeremy, no!"

I gave her a look over my shoulder. "Mom, I've got to be there."

We stared at each other.

"Just take Jamy home," I said.

"Don't talk to the police yet. Don't talk to anybody," she ordered. "Jeremy, promise."

"Okay."

She got into the car and took Jamy home and left me.

Running back to Aaron's house, I saw that Mrs. Gingrich was there, looking as white as her nurse uniform, standing with Mr. Gingrich, both of them looking lost even though they were right in front of their own house. Aaron's parents. I felt my insides go all clotted in my chest. I ran up to the yellow police tape, jumped it like a hurdle, and trotted up the yard.

Mr. Gingrich looked at me and said, "Son, how you doing?" like he barely knew what he was saying, like he might offer me a Popsicle or something, the way he always did when I went into his store. But Mrs. Gingrich choked out, "Oh, Jeremy," and kind of toppled toward me. The look on her face—I'd never seen her look like that, not even the time Aaron and I were poking around in the woodpile and Aaron got bit by a timber rattler. Then, when the doctors said he was going to be okay, she had cried and kidded around. Trust Aaron to find a rattlesnake in the backyard.

But now it was no joke and she wasn't crying. I think it was so bad, she couldn't cry.

I put my arms around her and said, "I'm sorry," which sounds really stupid but I didn't know what else to say. "I'm sorry."

She didn't make a sound or say a word, just held on to me like she was drowning, with her head on my shoulder. She nodded to show she'd heard me. I felt the movement against my collarbone. Maybe she couldn't talk.

Aardy and a couple of cops came out of the garage; they'd been talking with her in there, maybe? Somebody had given her a fistful of white Kleenex. Then a state cop came out of the house with his hand on the back of Nathan's neck, kind of guiding him along the sidewalk. Nathan's face looked flat white like a paper mask, and the stains on his shirt were red turning into purple and brown. He didn't look at me. I caught a glimpse of him, then turned my head away like I hadn't seen him.

The state trooper said to the Gingriches, "Come with me, folks," and Mrs. Gingrich let go of me. Herding Nathan and his parents toward the driveway, the cop jerked his head at me and gave me a look that told me to get lost. He motioned the Gingriches into his cruiser.

I went back to my place in the crowd and watched him drive the Gingriches away.

I stood in front of Aaron's house for hours. Afterward, Mom said she never should have let me stay, but I'm glad she did. It would have been even worse otherwise, imagining things. This way, I saw.

I saw the detectives drive up and walk in with their big black equipment cases. And the photographer. And the coroner. The plainclothes cops wore suit jackets, and the coroner wore a dress like she was going to church. And a droopy hat over her gray poodle curls. And thick nylons. Like, industrial-strength stockings. I guess they had to be thick for kneeling beside bodies.

I saw the sun shine lower and lower over the mountains. Shining, warm, when it should have gone cold and black. When it should have rained blood or something. I saw the coroner come out of the house again with her dress rumpled and her nylons wrinkled and her face sagging in deep lines. I saw the sky turn rosy colors and the sun go cherry red, sinking. I saw the photographer leave. It got so everything seemed like a creepy dream. I couldn't think who I was anymore or what I was doing there.

Finally, after dark, I saw the medics take Aaron out.

His body, I mean. They rolled it out on a gurney and loaded it onto the ambulance. They had it covered with a sheet, of course. But even though it had been hours, blood stained the cloth, looking black in the streetlamp light.

The ambulance rolled away, slow, no siren, no lights. Silent as a ghost.

The people who were left in the crowd turned away and went home, just as quiet. I stayed.

A couple of the uniformed township police stood at the bottom of the driveway talking to each other in hushed voices. I walked over to them, and they both swung their heads toward me and stared, as blank as the night.

I told them, "I've got to talk to somebody."

chapter three

One of the detectives took me home in his unmarked car with a laptop computer built into the console. He ran me on the computer and told me I didn't have any criminal history or any outstanding warrants. He was half joking, trying to lighten things up, but I couldn't smile. Maybe the look on my face was the same as the look on my mom's face when we walked in. I don't know. Probably, because Mom's face matched all the others I'd been seeing, stretched and pale like a drumhead.

The detective introduced himself and told Mom, "I want to take his statement in your presence, because he's a minor."

She looked at me. I told her, "It's okay." It wasn't okay, really. I felt like a murderer who couldn't wait to confess. I felt as bad as if I'd killed Aaron myself.

"I want you to talk with a lawyer first," Mom said.

"Mom, I already told him everything. He just needs to write it down."

The truth was, I'd told him everything except who Aaron had said he was afraid of. I wasn't going to snitch on Nathan, because he couldn't have done it. I mean, I'd known him as long as I'd known Aaron. When we were kids, we all played snow forts together, hunted fossils together in the abandoned strip mines, went camping and told ghost stories together. I remembered the time Nathan put a dead toad in my sleeping bag. I remembered getting in trouble with him and Aaron just about every Halloween for soaping windows and stuff. Okay, Nathan hadn't been hanging with us for the last couple of years, but all the same, I knew Nathan couldn't have done it. I just knew, like knowing which way is up.

The detective sat me at the kitchen table and got out a little tape recorder. Mom sat beside me with her lips pressed together, and I told it all again: Aaron had said he was scared and then wouldn't tell me why; he'd asked me to call and somebody had picked up and then the answering machine and then Nathan had said Aaron wasn't home. After a while Mom gave a sigh like she felt better and offered the detective a cup of coffee. He said no thanks, but was my sister around to verify what she knew?

The brat was up in her room, probably yakking with her preppy friends. Mom called her and she barefooted downstairs with her own precious cordless phone still in her hand. She looked like she'd been crying, yet enjoying the excitement. When she met the detective, she got big-eyed. He took her into the living room to talk with her. Mom went along.

I sat at the kitchen table trying not to look at the windows. Too dark. I'd never minded nighttime before, but that night I didn't like the darkness outside pressing the glass like it wanted in. I wanted to go somewhere but I didn't know where, or what to do, so I just sat there.

I could hear every word they said in the other room. "So your brother seemed upset?" the detective asked after the brat told him what time I'd come home, judging by what was on TV at the time, and what time she thought it was when I tried to phone Aaron.

"He acted majorly freaked."

"In what way—"

But the brat interrupted, all fluttery. "Is it true that somebody stabbed Aaron in the *face*?"

"I can't say, miss. I need the names—"

"They say it's a serial murderer. A psycho killer."

"Who says?"

"My friends."

"Do they know something I don't?" I could hear a teacher tone in his voice.

"No, I guess not, but—"

"Just rumors, miss. We don't know—"

"But is it true there was blood all over everything?"

I clenched my fists. Mom said, "Jamy, stop it."

The phone rang, and I got up and answered it.

"Jeremy!" It was a neighbor lady. "Mrs. Ledbetter says there's a police officer at your house asking questions. Is that true?"

I should have asked her what she needed a cop for, but I didn't know what to say. I felt so sick I mumbled, "'Scuse me," and hung up. Right away the phone rang again. It was like I had sunstroke or something, I felt so bad. I braced my hands on top of the table, stood there half bent over, and let the damn phone ring. Mom came out, looked at me, and took the phone off the hook without answering it. I heard the front door close as the detective left.

Jamy came in and said, "There's people in the front yard, and the TV van just pulled up."

"Good Lord," Mom said.

"What's the matter with Butthead?"

"Jamy, go to your room," Mom said, real sharp.

"Good grief, all I did was ask—"

"*Go.*"

Starting to feel a little better, I eased into a chair.

"Something to eat?" Mom asked. "Pizza?"

Jamy called down the stairs, "Mom, is the phone off the hook?"

"Yes, and now it's unplugged." She reached over and yanked the jack out of the wall. "Go to bed!"

"No!" Jamy yelled with panic in her voice. There was a silence while her fear hung in the air. Then she called more softly, "Can I sleep with you tonight?"

Somebody knocked at the door. Mom told Jamy, "Yes, I guess so," as she crossed the living room to look through the peephole. She turned away. "Don't answer. It's just reporters." She called up the stairs to Jamy, "Honey, I don't think anybody around here's going to get much sleep tonight."

"Can I come down?"

"Yes, if you leave your brother alone." Knock, knock, knock at the door. Ignoring it, Mom came back to me. "Something to eat, Jeremy?"

My gut felt as hollow as my sister's head, yet I couldn't have swallowed a bite if you paid me. "Can't," I said.

Her voice got softer. "You want to talk about it?"

I shook my head and stood up.

"Where are you going?"

"Out for a walk." Damn the stupid darkness.

"No."

I needed to get out of there so bad that for a minute I really hated her. My whole body clenched like a fist. "Mom, I—"

"Honey, I know, but you can't go out. We don't know what's out there."

"Except reporters," Jamy said.

She was supposed to leave me alone. I wanted to hit her. I wanted to hit something, kill something, kill whoever had killed Aaron, and the worst of it was, like Mom said, he was out there somewhere, and I didn't know where, and yeah, I was scared. I mean, I was Aaron's best friend—would I be next?

I was Aaron's best friend—shouldn't I do something?

Like what?

Damn it all to hell, I didn't know, and I needed to walk, run, shout, scream, throw something, smash something, bash something right that minute. I turned and lunged down the basement steps, slamming the door behind me.

I didn't even turn on a light at first, just blundered around down there, panting and hitting and flinging things. I threw a fit like a brat kid. I punched holes in cardboard boxes, heaved piles of newspapers into the air, swore until my voice started to break, and then I shut up because I was not going to cry, damn it I was not going to cry. I just fought with the dark.

After a while I wore myself out and just lay in a pile of newspaper, breathing hard and staring into nothing but blackness.

The door at the top of the stairs opened and light shot down. "Jeremy?"

"Let me alone, Mom."

"Are you all right?"

"Compared to what?"

I guess she could tell I was alive. The door closed.

Later I got up, flicked on a light, and looked at the mess I'd made. Jeez.

It was late but I knew I couldn't sleep. I couldn't think what else to do so I started to clean up.

After a while the door at the top of the stairs opened and Mom came down, still dressed. She didn't say a word, just started helping me.

"I'll get it," I said.

"I know," she said, but she kept picking up newspapers. She stacked them and tied them up as carefully as if she were wrapping Christmas presents, taking her time. And then, I couldn't believe this, here came Jamy in sweats and slippers, and she started picking up, too, quiet, like Mom.

After we got the mess cleared away, I got out the shop vac and Mom got a broom and Jamy got a dust cloth. All that night we hardly said a word, and we cleaned that basement till you could have held a reception there.

chapter four

What with no sleep, in the morning I was kind of floating, spaced out and limp enough so I could eat, even though I still didn't really feel hungry. I was working my way through a bowl of Frosted Flakes at the kitchen table, with Mom sipping coffee across from me, when the brat headed for the living room and I heard the TV click on. The morning news anchor was saying, ". . . and a murder stuns Pinto River."

I yelled, "Jamy, turn it off!"

"No way."

"Listen, frog face—"

"Booger, deal with it." But her voice was quiet, and I shut up, because Booger was what Aaron called me. I mean, other people did, too, but he was the one who started it. Fourth grade. He caught me picking my nose, a big green one, and he grabbed my wrist and flicked my hand and the booger flew up and hung on the ceiling over my desk. I was never so embarrassed in my life, and I just about hated him. I mean, in a movie they couldn't have done it better. Everybody who was in that class still remembered.

Except Aaron. He was dead.

Oh, my God. What was I going to do without him? I mean, I'm nothing. Two ears, two eyes, nose in the middle of my face. Average looks, average grades, I'm so average it hurts. I'm Jeremy Nobody. But just because Aaron was my friend, that made me somebody.

". . . Pinto River's first murder since 1976," the announcer was saying.

"Good grief," Mom said, "that was before you were born. Man shot his girlfriend." She wasn't really talking to me, just remembering. "Turned himself in," she said, and she went to watch the news with Jamy. I stayed where I was, trying to finish my cereal, listening.

". . . youthful victim. Aaron Gingrich, seventeen, a popular student and starting halfback on Pinto River Area High School's championship-winning football team, was found dead in his home yesterday . . ."

Maybe Dad would give me a call, I thought. He knew Aaron was my best friend. And even if he didn't watch the news he would have heard all about the murder at his hangout, the Tipple Tavern, since the cops all hung there too. Or he'd hear about it at the courthouse where he worked. I hoped he'd call.

"There's Jeremy," Jamy said. "Hey, Jeremy," she called, "you're on TV."

"Shut up!" I guess they were showing the house and the crowd, and I never wanted less to see myself on TV.

The news kept blabbing. Cause of death was "multiple stab wounds to the neck." Around that point I gave up on my cereal and tried not to listen anymore, but I still heard. They said that Cecily had found Aaron's body. She'd been at a friend's house—"That's us!" Jamy squealed like it made her famous—and, upon returning home, had found her brother lying dead approximately ten feet inside the front door, in the living room. They said Nathan, who had been upstairs sleeping, had come down when he heard his sister screaming, then phoned 911. They said both Cecily and Nathan were in shock and under a doctor's care. The family was in seclusion with relatives. Nothing appeared to be missing from the Gingrich home, and there was no sign of forced entry.

Pinto River had beefed up police patrols, and the school system, due to begin classes next week, was opening its doors early to students in need of help dealing with the tragedy. Trained counselors would be on hand. . . .

When they started talking about the weather, hot with thunderstorms, Mom came back into the kitchen and poured herself more coffee. "I'm taking off work," she said, which was something; Mom never took off work. The quarry just about can't run without her. But she said, "I'm worthless today. I'm going to bed. So is Jamy. Jeremy, are you going to try to get some sleep?"

I shook my head. Didn't want to go to bed till I was sure I'd be out like a light, not lying there with Aaron on my mind and wondering if maybe I was next. Anyway, being falling-down tired kind of helped. I couldn't think much or feel much.

Mom stared at me. "What are you doing, then?"

"You're not going to believe this." Because it was, like, optional.

"What?"

"I'm going to school."

The high school lobby was crowded and freaky quiet. Mostly kids my age, seniors, and they should have been yelling and tossing Super Balls around and girls should have been prancing and squealing and giggling and guys should have been grinning and punching each other in the shoulder, but they all stood talking softly like old people in church. When I walked in, they even stopped talking. Everybody looked at me. Then a girl named Morgan kind of choked out, "Booger, hi," and ran to me and hugged me, and all my friends crowded around. Two other girls hugged me. My feelings came back to life, and I hurt bad.

"Hey, Boog." A couple of the guys reached over to whack my back. I couldn't say anything.

"My mom says you're in the morning paper, man," one of the guys said. I looked at him, and he explained. "Last known person to see him alive."

31

"Great," I said, "just wonderful," and I turned away. Wandered to the middle of the lobby and stood there with freaky, quiet talk all around me.

". . . couldn't sleep. Like, whoever did it, he's out there somewhere."

". . . my stepfather went out and bought a gun . . ."

"Who would want to kill Aaron? I mean . . ."

". . . if there was somebody in there and he walked in on them . . . but why . . ."

". . . got to be a psycho who came in from the interstate or something."

". . . blood all over the place. They say his head was almost cut off."

". . . thinks Nathan did it."

I went cold. And I guess I wasn't the only one, because there was this frozen silence. Then Morgan added, "I didn't say he did it! I just said my mom thinks he did."

Some guy growled, "Your mom's a stupid bitch, then."

"Thank you. I'll tell her you said so."

A bunch of kids started talking at once, mostly saying Nathan couldn't have done it. Like, it had to be a stranger, not somebody we knew. But one of the guys on the debate team was loudest. "Anyone who thinks Nathan did it ought to be hung by the ears!"

Morgan said, "Everybody's entitled to their opinion. What if Nathan, like, lost it—"

Like listening to a stranger I heard myself say, "For

God's sake, Morgan, Aaron was strong as a Mack truck, and Nathan was smaller. Is, I mean. He weighs less. Why would Aaron let him—"

"I don't know!" Morgan glared back at me like she was about to cry. "I don't know what happened, I'm just saying—"

"Why don't you just shut up?" I turned away.

"Hey, Jeremy," some girl called, "we're going to get some flowers. Want to come?"

It wasn't like I'd walked all the way to school to talk to some shrink. I did it because I wanted to be with my friends and the other kids. So sure, no problem, I went along with a bunch of girls to the farm market and helped pay for about six kinds of flowers and then we all went to Aaron's place. I sat in the middle of the backseat feeling really weird as we drove into my development. The girls were busy making the flowers into a bouquet for each of us. Fine, good, whatever. Girls were good at this kind of thing, and I was not. I wasn't worth a damn at anything. I could have saved Aaron, and I should have, and now he was dead and I didn't know what to do.

"There," somebody said in a whisper, and we pulled up near Aaron's house.

It was like a snowplow had gone along the road and left a big drift in front of the Gingrich place, except it wasn't snow; it was flowers. All along the street and the edge of the lawn under the yellow police tape, bunches of flowers four feet deep, mostly white. Even before I got out of the car, I could smell them like some woman had put on too much perfume. After I laid my bouquet down, I stood there looking at all of them. All those flowers, and notes people had left to tell the Gingrich family they were praying for them, and a cake in the shape of a football, and some real footballs lying in the flowers like oversize brown Easter eggs. And some white wooden crosses, even though Aaron never gave a doo-dah-day about religion. And big posters that said AARON, WE'LL MISS YOU, AARON, WE LOVE YOU.

It was all so useless. So stupid. Like me.

"We ought to take a photo for the yearbook," one of the girls said.

Like that would do any good? I walked away from them, and now I didn't even feel like going back to the school. I was about to walk home when I heard the house door open. I looked up and the detective who had taken me home last night was coming out, lugging a big white plastic bag. He called, "Jeremy, wait," and walked down the driveway to talk with me.

"How you doing?" he asked.

"Okay."

"You sure?"

"No."

He smiled a little. "You going to get some counseling?"

"No." What was the use? I changed the subject. "What's that?" I asked, looking at the bag.

"Carpet sample for the lab. Listen, Jeremy, I was just talking to your mom," he said. "We want you to come in for a polygraph reading."

"Huh? Polygraph?"

"Some people call it a lie detector, but it's not really. It's—"

"I didn't lie to you!" I burst out. I really hadn't lied, just left one thing out.

He looked at me kind of funny. "It's a routine informational reading, not anything official. Not admissible in court, like a statement. It's just to help us sort things out. Everyone concerned with this case is taking a polygraph test."

"My sister?" I asked.

"Yes, and the other girls as well."

"Nathan?"

"I can't divulge that."

I walked home and let myself in the back door. The house was quiet. A note on the kitchen table said Mom and the brat were sleeping. I didn't want to sleep yet. Went to the bathroom and washed my face with cold water and glanced at the mirror over the sink. Funny, the way my mind was swimming, I expected to see me with gray hair like the coroner's. But I looked just the same as before.

chapter five

I thought of calling off work that night, but then what would I do? Sit around the house and pick my nose? So I drank coffee to force my eyes open and then I went. I guess Mom figured I was okay to drive, because she let me take the car, but maybe her judgment wasn't so great that day. When I punched in, Rose took one look at me and said, "You're on counter. I don't want you driving deliveries." Rose is tough and nice. Owns the place, Rose's Italian Café and Take-Out. Three square tables and a bench, red and green tile on the walls, pictures pasted together out of colored macaroni.

A sign over the door says, BEST FOOD IN PINTO RIVER. Actually, it's the only food in Pinto River. Besides Rose's café, there's the GGG, Gingrich's Grocery and General Store, which is where you can usually find Mr. Gingrich, though I guess not today. And there's the church, Pinto River Presbyterian, and a gas station, and a video rental place, and a woman who does haircuts in her kitchen, and that's about it, except some old houses with plaster deer in front, and the school complex, and my development. The nearest real town, with a Cinemax and a Wal-Mart, is twenty miles away.

Usually when I work at Rose's I do delivery, and I get good tips that way. I hate counter because hardly anybody tips and some people are really rude.

That night, every single person who came in wanted to talk about Aaron. The murder, I mean. They'd make comments to me, like, "He was your friend, wasn't he, Jeremy?" and my gut would twist itself into a granny knot and all I could do was nod and say, "You want cheese on that?"

It wasn't any better when they didn't know me and just talked among themselves. "I heard they finished the autopsy," one old guy said to his wife, girlfriend, whatever, while they were sitting on the bench waiting for their stromboli. "I heard they counted seventy-three slices and stab wounds."

"*How* many?" Her voice went shrill.

"Seventy-three."

"How can they *count* that many in just his neck?"

"I don't know. They say his head was just about cut off. They say whoever it was kept stabbing him after he was dead. They hacked right through his spine, just left a thread of skin at the back of his neck."

I ducked down behind the counter, pretending I was looking for something, so they wouldn't see my face. I felt like I was going to puke.

It didn't help that some guy called across the room to them, "There were lots of cuts in his hands and arms, I heard. Like he flung up his hands trying to defend himself."

The woman said, "I heard it was awful. All that blood. They wouldn't let his parents look at him. I heard even the cops couldn't stand to look at him. One cop threw up."

I ran for the john. After I came out, Rose asked me, "You sick?"

"Not anymore."

She came over and kind of smoothed my forehead with her big beefy hand. Her hand felt hot like a toaster, I was so sweaty cold. She said, "You need to go home?"

I shook my head.

"You *want* to go home?"

I shook my head again.

"You'd rather be here?"

I nodded. Anything was better than hanging around the house.

"Okay, then get back to work."

The guy across the room was saying, "I guess they're going to have a closed casket funeral service, huh? Can't have a viewing if he's carved up like that."

"I dunno," the shrill woman said. "Them under-takers can do wonders with wax. Give them photos, they can make it look just like him."

"Not after the coroners get done with him. They do

an autopsy, they gotta take out his heart, liver, brain, everything."

I ran for the john again.

By the end of the night I got done heaving, but people never got done talking. The worst was when two old women came in for subs. "Veggie on wheat, no mayonnaise," one of them said to me, and then she said to her friend, "The way I figure, he was probably mixed up in drugs. These kids out at the high school, they're all high on drugs all the time."

I was a high school kid, and I wasn't high on drugs. I was waiting on her. I asked her, "American cheese or provolone?"

"American," she told me, and she told her friend, "They do drugs and then they kill things with knives. Satanic rites."

Her friend said, "But wouldn't you think the parents would've noticed something?"

"But all these broken homes, and then the parents both work, that's the thing. Money, money, money, and the kids raise themselves."

The second woman nodded hard. "They all smoke dope these days, all the time. They're not interested in improving themselves. No work ethic—"

"And what can I get for you, ma'am?" I asked her.

"Seafood salad on white with oil and vinegar, lots of lettuce and tomato, no mayo, no cheese. And put a little salt on it. And just a dash of that there Old Bay seasoning." She went on talking with the first one. "What I mean, it's a shame he died, but I bet that boy's room is full of drugs. No work and all play, parties and drugs, the way they act, they deserve to get killed."

I was so tired I didn't even know how I felt anymore, but I guess some sort of noise choked itself out of my throat. Both women stared at me, and one of them said, "What's the matter with you, young man?"

I whispered, "Is that for here or to go?"

I don't really believe in ghosts or angels or the afterlife or any of that, but when I finally lay down in my bed, I would have sworn I heard Aaron calling me. Like he was right outside the front door, and he was yelling, "Jeremy! BOOGER! Let me in!" He was real upset, I could tell by his voice, but I was so tired I couldn't move. I hurt all over with wanting to help him, but at the same time I was scared of him because he was dead, which made him, like, a different person. Like I didn't know him anymore. Like he had to be full of hate, like he might hurt me. Yet he was still Aaron, my buddy, and I wanted to go to him, and at the same time I wanted to run away, and I wanted to cry, and I couldn't do any of it. All I could do was lie there like lead while he yelled, "Booger! You were supposed to call me, man! Why didn't you call when I told you to?" Way pissed off. But really, I think it was *me* pissed off at me. I mean,

I know it was all in my head. Maybe I was so worn out I was hallucinating. Maybe I was already asleep, dreaming.

But at the time it seemed so damn real I wanted to pee my pants. Now I know why people think there are ghosts.

Next day around noon I woke up and couldn't remember for a minute why I felt so awful. Then it hit me all over again. Aaron. Dead.

I just lay there. Couldn't face the day. After a while the pain eased up, I started to drift, and I daydreamed Aaron was still alive, he was okay, I had saved him. I had phoned at just the right minute to distract the murderer so Aaron could run out the door. Or, no, I had followed Aaron home because I knew something was going to happen, I heard him yell and I ran into his house like rushing a quarterback and there was this huge guy in a black ski mask lunging at Aaron with the knife and I kicked the knife out of his hand and he hollered and turned on me and Aaron got away and I tackled the murderer and he went down and I kicked him and kicked him—

There I lay in bed, punching the pillow and kicking the mattress. I could daydream all I liked, but Aaron was still dead.

It took me an hour to get myself together and pointed in a direction and moving. Finally I got up, showered, found something to wear, and sat down in the kitchen to eat a leftover sub Rose had sent home with me. Mom was at work, I guess. She had left a big Hallmark sympathy card on the table with a note for me to sign it so she could send it to the Gingriches. She and Jamy had already signed it, and Mom had written a little note saying how sorry she was. The card said about the same, except it rhymed.

I wanted to write something, and I tried to think what. I mean, the Gingriches were like a second family to me, especially when Mom and Dad broke up. I remembered sleeping over there for two or three days at a time, and Mrs. Gingrich would make homemade macaroni and cheese and not ask too many questions. Mr. Gingrich helped Mom with my shoes and stuff for football, got them wholesale. He and Mrs. Gingrich both saw us through a hard time. But now that Aaron was dead, I couldn't think of what to say to either of them. Or Aardy. Or Nathan.

I signed my name, but I didn't write any note.

I tried to eat the rest of the sub, but I couldn't. I threw it in the garbage, then headed out to go take my polygraph test.

chapter six

I'd never been in the police station before, and when I got to the front door, I felt freaked, like I was a criminal or something. I had to force myself to haul on the handle and keep going. But once I got inside, it wasn't like a TV jail or anything, more like a doctor's office, with a waiting room and a receptionist at a desk behind a sliding-glass window. Not that I like doctor's offices too much, either, but the receptionist didn't keep me waiting. She called the detective, and then she led me into the back, which was just a bunch of grubby offices that smelled like cigarette smoke, and a dark little locker room with the door hanging open, and a room with shelves and coatracks and six old typewriters. The receptionist pointed me into the detective's office.

The detective wasn't scary, either, just a skinny little guy with bright eyes, interested in everything, including me. He sat me down in a chair with ripped plastic uphol-stery, gave me a pen and a clipboard, and helped me fill out medical history forms and consent forms and stuff.

We talked for more than an hour. He wanted to make sure I understood about the polygraph, that I had to answer all the questions either yes or no, that he'd run the same test three times to make sure, that none of this was evidence. I wanted to ask him, what was it, then? But we got to talking about football, and somehow we ended up talking about Aaron and Nathan and me. I told him about one time when we were little kids, we played mailman and switched around all the mail in all the mailboxes in the neighborhood. He laughed so hard, he got me laughing. I wouldn't have believed I could still laugh. I liked him. I asked, "Are you really a cop?"

"Sure. I'm a detective."

"You like it?"

"Yeah, it's really interesting. I get to meet a lot of people this way, and most of them are great folks who just have to come in here because something bad happened. Like you."

I wondered whether he knew my father. A lot of the cops do, because Dad works courthouse security. But just as I thought of asking, the detective said, "C'mon, I'll show you the polygraph."

He led me out of his office to another room—a bare little brown room with no window, and a bench screwed to one wall with a big steel pipe mounted above it, like, for handcuffs, and a big steel ring in the floor. I took one look at that place and I froze.

The detective gave me a smile. "We do it in here because it's quiet. No distractions, no interruptions."

He closed the door behind us, and yeah, it sure was quiet.

"Here it is," he said, and I got myself turned around to look. Against the wall opposite the handcuff bar and stuff was a plain table with a big black machine on it.

The detective beckoned. "C'mere, I'll show you how it works. All it does is measure your physiological response . . ." He showed me the ink bottles—red, blue, and black—and the needles and the graph paper the machine kept inching out. He sat me down in a folding chair and hooked me up: a black tube thing around my chest to measure my breathing, a cuff like the one they use in a doctor's office on my arm to measure my blood pressure and my pulse, and little tubes on two of my fingers to measure my skin reflex. At that point I said, "Huh?"

"Your skin's an organ, just like your heart or your lungs—"

"It is?"

"Yeppers. And it responds . . . well, for starters, it puts out sweat, right?"

It sure did. I was sweating already.

"I have to establish a baseline first," he said. "We'll run a trial strip, okay? I want you to close your eyes and think of a number between one and five."

45

Whatever. I chose the number two. I sat there with my eyes closed thinking *two* and feeling him inflate the cuff on my arm.

"Okay," I heard him say, "I want you to answer 'no' to each question, all right? In other words, I want you to lie. Here we go." A pause, then he asked. "Of the number you chose between one and five, was it number one?"

"No."

Another pause.

"Of the number you chose between one and five, was it number two?"

"No."

He went on till five, then said, "Okay, you can open your eyes. Was it number two?"

"Yeah, it was!" I gawked at him. It was just a stupid trial, for God's sake, not a real lie, and I hadn't felt myself sweat or anything.

"Do you want to see?" he asked.

I looked at the graph paper. He had marked the numbers on the edge. At number two, all four lines jumped.

"There's your physiological response," he said. "Fascinating, isn't it?"

Yeah. Fascinating. Uh-huh.

"Okay, now that I have an idea of your normal response, I'm going to ask you to close your eyes again. . . ."

He asked easy questions at first, like, was my name Jeremy Matthew Davis? Yes. Was I seventeen years old?

Yes. Questions like that, and then he eased into the real questions. Was I friends with Aaron Gingrich? Yes. Had we gone bike riding the day Aaron was murdered? Yes. And so on, everything I had told the first detective.

"Did Nathan answer the third phone call?"

"Yes."

"Did he identify himself as Nathan?"

"No."

"Did you recognize his voice?"

"Yes."

"At that time, did Nathan say Aaron was not home?"

"Yes."

"To the best of your knowledge, was the time of that call approximately 5:15 P.M.?"

"Yes."

"Do you know who killed Aaron Gingrich?"

"No."

"Did Aaron tell you who he was afraid of?"

My heart lurched. "No."

"Jeremy, is there anything pursuant to the death of Aaron Gingrich that you are not telling me?"

"No." Sweating.

"Okay. You can open your eyes." He deflated the cuff on my arm. "Do you want to take a break before we do it again?"

Yeah, I sure did. I could see the last couple of questions on the graph paper, my lines jumping practically off the edge, but he didn't say a word about it. He didn't

47

say anything after I came back from the bathroom, either, just hooked me up and we did it all over again. The exact same questions. I started sweating before he even got to the one . . .

"Did Aaron tell you who he was afraid of?"

I tried to say no, but I knew it was no use. I bent over in my chair and hugged my head in my hands.

The detective said, "Jeremy?"

"Oh, shit."

I think he shut off the machine, and then, I swear to God, he hunkered down in front of me and put his hands on top of mine—his hands felt warm. He said, "Open your eyes, son. Look at me." I did, and I saw nothing in his face except sympathy. "Just spit it out," he said. "Who was Aaron afraid of?"

"Nathan," I whispered.

"What, exactly, did Aaron say?"

By then I understood what a polygraph machine was for. After he got the whole story out of me, he nodded, stood up, and started to take the tubes and stuff off me. He asked, "Why didn't you tell us that before?"

"Because Nathan didn't do it! He couldn't have!"

"That's for the investigators and the jury to decide, son, not you or me. What you've done is called withholding evidence, and that's a crime under the law. I'm not going to file charges against you, but I could."

Not even trying to be smart, I said, "Honest to God, I really don't care."

He eyed me, then nodded as if he understood. "Start caring again," he said. "Have you been beating up on yourself, son?"

"Huh?"

The word hurt. *Huh, hell, pay attention,* Aaron would have said.

The detective said, "Have you been telling yourself you could have saved him?"

What the hell, did this guy have ESP? I stared at him, and I guess he saw the answer in my face. He nodded.

"Probably you couldn't have done a damn thing," he said. "When you're in my business, you see that trying to be a hero doesn't stick it. They say hindsight's 20/20 but really most of the time it's a liar. Wishful thinking."

"Really?"

"Really. So don't you put yourself down, son. You're just a good kid, doing your best, like most of us. I want you to remember that."

He made it sound like an order. I nodded.

"You got to take care of yourself," he said, "because things are going to get worse before they get better."

chapter seven

He was right about that.

Close to midnight the phone rang. I was actually sleeping, too, damn it. Whenever anybody phones late, it's usually for me, so I stumbled out of bed. Actually, I was hoping it was Dad, calling late because he keeps strange hours. I barged into the brat's room, where she was lying like a lump upside down on her bed, with her head where her feet should have been, and I grabbed her phone. " 'Lo?"

It wasn't Dad. A man's polite voice said, "Is this Jeremy Davis?"

"Yeah."

"You goddamn liar, you ought to be shot." It was so sudden, the way his voice turned from polite to hateful, I just stood there stunned like he'd really put a bullet in me, which was stupid. I mean, I should have known something like this might happen. It's impossible to keep anything to yourself in Pinto River. That detective had to tell other cops, and the way this town works, he might as well have used a megaphone. Of course everybody knew. And now they were taking sides, and everybody who was friends with the Gingriches hated me. I half hated myself.

The guy on the phone snarled, "No, shooting's too good for you, lying snitch. As if that poor family don't have trouble enough already. Ain't you got no decency?"

Apparently all the decent people of Pinto River just absolutely *knew* that some outsider killed Aaron.

The guy told me, "I hope the psycho who killed that poor boy does you the same way."

I dropped the phone like it was a timber rattlesnake, but I could still hear the guy shouting. My lump sister must have heard too, because she rolled to the edge of her bed, snagged the phone off the floor, said into it, "Get a life," and hung up. "Jeez," she said.

The phone rang again. From Mom's room came her sleepy, grouchy voice. "Jeremy, who the—"

I hollered, "Mom, you answer it!"

"Just let it ring!" Jamy yelled.

"*What?*" As the phone kept ringing, Mom showed up at the bedroom door, pulling her bathrobe on. "Who?"

I didn't know how to explain, so I picked up the phone and handed it to her. It was the same guy. I could hear him from where I stood. Mom's face changed, and she said, "Sir, I am going to call the police." But he just got louder. Mom hung up on him and pulled out the phone jack. She looked at me. "What's he talking about?"

She'd asked me at supper how the polygraph went, but I'd just rolled my eyes at her and asked her to pass the ketchup. Didn't want to talk about it. Now I mumbled, "My guess is, I was in the late news."

Jamy said, "Huh?" and sat up staring at me.

Mom said, "For what?"

"For what the damn lie detector made me say, damn it."

"Excuse me?"

"Aaron said—" I could barely get it out. "That day—when Aaron said he was scared—I asked him what was the matter, and he said—" I couldn't go on.

"He said *what*?" Jamy demanded.

Mom told me, kind of like the detective, "Jeremy, just take a deep breath and spit it out."

I whispered, "Nathan."

For a minute Mom and Jamy just stared. Then Jamy said, "Oh . . . my . . . God."

And Mom did something I never expected. She walked over and hugged me.

I didn't want anybody touching me. I yelped, "Mom, get off."

She stood back. "I was just thinking of the Gingriches," she said, her voice wavery. "Those poor people, they've lost a child, and . . . and they might lose another . . ."

The Gingriches. Memories. Mrs. Gingrich baking snickerdoodles for Halloween, handing me a plateful warm out of the oven and saying, "Jeremy, sample these for me, would you, and see if they're any good?" Knowing darn well I'd eat every one of them. Then Mr. Gingrich coming in and saying, "Eat up, son. How did practice go today?"

Oh, my God.

It hit me like a rock, what I'd done to them. I guess I'd been kind of hoping the Gingriches wouldn't have to know.

Mom said, "Jeremy? You okay?"

I whispered, "They're going to hate me."

Mom sighed, then said quietly, "Probably. But you had to tell the truth. You should have told the truth to start with."

The brat butted in. "That's really what Aaron said? He was afraid of Nathan?"

"Yes, damn it! Shut up!"

"Jeremy!" Mom hushed me. "Shhhh."

But my stupid sister didn't shhhh. She kind of squeaked, "Oh, my God, what if Aardy . . . Oh my God, I've *got* to talk with her." Like she hadn't been leaving messages on the Gingriches' answering machine for a couple of days?

"You can't, honey." Mom sounded very tired.

"But what if . . . what if she saw something, or she knows something. . . ."

Mom said sharply, "Jamy, don't even go there."

"But what if she's scared?"

The kitchen phone started ringing.

"Shut up," I whispered.

Mom said, "I'll get it. I'll pull the plug, I mean. Jamy, honey, there's nothing you can do for your friend. I'm sorry. Don't think about it anymore tonight. You either, sweetie." She looked at me. "It's no use worrying. Just try to get some sleep."

Yeah. Right.

I heard every noise the rest of the night, including the newspaper hitting the door at five in the morning. At which point I muttered, "Damn it to hell," got out of bed, and headed downstairs. I made coffee, got the paper in, and started reading it to see what, exactly, people were saying about me. I still couldn't quite handle watching the news on TV but I could read the damn paper. And there I was, front page news: "Friend Implicates Gingrich Brother." Oh, just great. Lovely. The Gingrich family had issued a statement through their lawyer saying the police investigation was a farce and calling for an attorney general's investigation and apprehension of the real killer. Nathan had been taken in for questioning. There was a picture of Nathan and his father and a lawyer going into the police station, but not hiding their faces under their jackets or anything. Nathan had a fresh buzz cut and he was staring straight ahead.

I didn't know my mother was behind me, reading over my shoulder, till she said, "It's not the first time they had him in for questioning."

I jumped. "Huh?"

Huh, hell, pay attention. Aaron's voice in my mind. I had to close my eyes.

Mom was saying, "Nathan's the chief suspect, I think. They questioned him before."

"That's stupid! He couldn't have done it." What I meant was, not the Nathan I knew.

"I'm just telling you."

"It's some kind of weird coincidence. A mistake. Somebody told Aaron a lie or something." And I'd repeated it and made it worse, and now the police were looking the wrong way while the real murderer was still out there.

Mom said, "We all believe what we have to, Jeremy." Whatever that meant. I didn't ask; she didn't say. She pulled yesterday's newspaper off the top of the fridge, laid it in front of me, and got herself coffee.

There must have been three or four different articles about the murder in each paper. "I don't want to read all this stuff," I said.

Mom sighed. "It wouldn't hurt you to read for a change." But then she sat down across from me and said, "When they searched the house, they found some very graphic images of violence in his room. Printed off the Internet, maybe."

So what? Nathan had always liked horror movies, gory posters, that kind of thing. "That doesn't mean—"

"I know, but it makes you wonder."

"Did they find, um—"

"Drugs? No. Not a trace of drugs anywhere in the house."

"That's not what I meant." Jeez, what was it with old people and drugs? "Did they find, you know, the knife—"

"The murder weapon? Yes. A bayonet. Thrown into the sump hole in the basement."

"Was it, like, a hunting knife or what?"

"They won't say."

"Where'd it come from? The house?"

"Won't say."

"Fingerprints on it?"

"They won't say that either."

They wouldn't say this, they wouldn't say that—I wished they wouldn't have said I blabbed, then. Though my name wasn't actually in the paper. But hell, there were people in Pinto River whose whole profession in life was to find out who did what and then tell anyone who hadn't already heard. Everybody was going to know it was me.

I didn't want to talk anymore, so I pretended I was reading. I scanned a few articles. There was an editorial about how Nathan had no criminal record and no history of mental illness and did okay in school and distinguished himself on the debate team and belonged to a nice middle-class churchgoing family, the point being that kids like me who slept in on Sunday morning looked more like a murderer than Nathan did, I guess.

Then there was an article where some guy tried to say what had happened in the Gingrich house. He said Aaron had put his bike away, then he'd no sooner walked in the door from the garage than he had come up against the killer with the knife. Then, according to the blood trail, Aaron had run to the front door, where he got stabbed some more trying to get out, and then he'd headed toward his room but he didn't make it, and then . . . I couldn't read about it anymore.

I switched over to another article, this one about techniques of criminal investigation and all the gadgets the Pinto River detectives had borrowed from the state police and how the black light machine could see blood even after it was wiped up. Blood could never be totally washed away, it said. Even if you scrubbed it with bleach, even if you painted over it, even after years went by, there would always be some stain, some trace of a blood trail.

I pushed the newspaper away. Mom got up for her second cup of coffee and plugged the phone back in.

It rang.

"Let the answering machine pick up," Mom said.

We both sat there listening to the phone ring. Three rings, four. Jamy bawled down in a sleepy voice, "Would somebody *get* it?"

The machine got it, and it was a woman this time, her voice like poison. "I just want you people to know you deserve to die like that boy did. As if it ain't bad enough without you spreading lies—"

I said, "Yank it again, Mom."

She shook her head. "The stupid woman's putting herself on tape for the police. And I do intend to call the police. We don't have to put up with this." She said to the phone, "Keep talking, honey."

I stood up and headed outside to get away. Bad move. The minute I closed the door behind me, old Mrs. Ledbetter across the street popped out, waved, and yodeled, "Yoo-hoo, Jeremy!" I figured she wanted me to do something for her, because the only time she usually yoo-hooed me was if she wanted me to mow her lawn or whatever. I sighed, waved back, and trudged on over there.

She walked down her lawn to meet me, short and round and dressed brighter than her petunias in candy-pink polyester with pink sneakers to match. "Jeremy," she asked when I got close enough to talk to, "how are you doing?"

"Um, okay." I was kind of surprised, because she never usually cared how I was doing. I looked at her, and she looked back at me with pale old eyes kind of naked between lids without any eyelashes.

"I realize you and Aaron were good friends," she said.

I wondered whether she knew Aaron used to say she looked like an Easter egg. She was trying to be nice, I could tell, but I didn't want to talk. I just nodded.

"Have the police told you anything?" she asked.

Oh. Okay. Maybe Mrs. Ledbetter had feelings about what had happened but she was still basically functioning as a database, Pinto River Info Central. I shook my head and started to turn away, but she put out one of her little round paws to stop me.

"Jeremy," she told me, "I know you're a nice boy, but some people just don't think. Have they been giving you a hard time?"

"Um, gotta go, Mrs. Ledbetter," I muttered.

I U-turned back into the house.

Once I got the front door locked behind me I just leaned against it and closed my eyes. Mrs. Ledbetter meant to be my friend, but in my mind I could hear her on the phone right this minute, telling her buddies that she saw Jeremy Davis and he wouldn't talk and he looked awful, all upset. And they would call people they knew and tell them—what? That they heard Jeremy Davis wouldn't talk? By the time it got around town, some of them would be saying I had something to hide. Jeremy Davis looked awful? What's that mean? Grieving? Or guilty?

By the time they got done, some of them would be saying I killed Aaron myself.

Damn phones anyway. Mom was on ours talking with the cops about the threatening calls. When she was finished, and when I was sure she was in the bathroom and she wouldn't hear me, I called my father.

But he wasn't home. Story of my life. I left a message on his answering machine: "Dad, hi, this is Jeremy. Would you do me a favor? I want you to get me a gun."

chapter eight

"Hold your head up, son," Mom told me softly as we walked to the church door for Aaron's funeral.

Easier said than done, when I'd been getting hate calls for three days. When people who didn't even know me were saying I was a lying bastard lower than dog doo. When I was wearing a suit and I felt dressed up like a circus monkey. When there were news photographers climbing the trees to snap pictures of me. When even the stony old mountains seemed to be watching me. But screw all that. I did what Mom said. I yanked my eyes off the pavement and looked around as we reached the end of the line waiting to go in.

People looked at me, then looked away like they didn't know what to do or say. Three guys from the football team walked over to me and muttered, "Hi, Booger," then stood beside me looking the same way.

A few people glared. "Dirty liar," taunted a girl's voice from the crowd.

"None of that, miss," growled one of the cops at the

door. There were uniformed police everywhere. Crowd control, I guess. School had started today, but seniors had the day off to attend Aaron's funeral. Nearly everybody in my class was there, and it seemed like nearly everybody in Pinto River was there, too. To show sympathy for the family? Or to gawk at them and at me?

The guys from the team kind of drifted away.

". . . should be ashamed to show his face," muttered a man's voice in the crowd.

"In this country it's innocent until proved guilty," said some woman quietly, and I couldn't tell whether she was talking about me or Nathan.

That was what really freaked me. Most people, the ones keeping their distance, I couldn't tell what they were really thinking. Like, were they just embarrassed? Or trying to stay in good with the Gingriches? Or did they really despise me? All around me and especially behind me I heard people mumbling to each other—about me?

I felt a big warm hand on my shoulder, turned around, and there was Coach from school. "Jeremy," he said, "how you doing, son?"

All of a sudden I got choked up and couldn't answer. But my sister was standing there and she said, "He's being a total boogerhead."

Coach smiled. "Good." He said to my mom, "Okay if I sit with you folks?"

"Jeremy." Another voice, a girl's, and there stood Morgan, looking at me kind of puzzled. "What made you change your mind?"

Oh. Jeez. I was the one who had yelled at *her* to shut up about Nathan. I told her, "I'm not sure I even have a mind. Listen, I'm sorry—"

"Forget it." All of a sudden she gave me a hug, then headed away.

"That's Jeremy Davis," whispered a voice behind me. "What's *he* doing here?" I didn't turn around.

Once we finally got inside, it was dim and crowded and way quiet. Hushed. All those people making barely a sound. That silence made me feel like I couldn't get enough air. Or maybe it was the too-sweet smell from an avalanche of flowers up front.

Around the casket.

Other than zillions of flowers, and candles burning to keep him company, Aaron was lying there all by himself in the closed casket. There hadn't been any viewing. No chance to say good-bye, but no need to see Aaron all hacked up, either. I imagined him the way I remembered him, round-faced and shiny-eyed, lying in that glorified polyurethane-and-wood box with gold doodads. It probably had puffy satin lining, too. He would have laughed at it.

Just inside the door, a man turned to me and shook my hand; it was the bright-eyed little detective who'd busted the truth out of me. "How are you doing these days?"

"Like you said," I told him. Maybe he'd heard. A couple days ago the cops were letting the Gingriches get some stuff out of their house, and I'd tried to talk with Mrs. Gingrich, but she'd slammed the door in my face. Jamy had gotten the same treatment when she'd tried to ask how Aardy was doing.

I told the detective, "You called it. Getting worse by the day."

"Yeah, but then it'll get better again. Hang in."

Gray-suited undertaker guys were packing people in, but all the pews were crammed butt to butt now. Aaron would have made some kind of joke about that, too, people cheek to cheek but not slow-dancing. . . . My eyes fogged up. Damn, where was Aaron now when I needed him? Dumb clown, why did he have to go and get killed? I felt like I was never going to laugh anymore, without Aaron around.

I could see Mrs. Ledbetter up front—she must have claimed her seat practically at dawn. Mom and Jamy and I didn't get to sit down. We stood against the back wall, and Coach stood with us, even though most of the guys from the football team had kind of clustered along one side.

After a while the Gingrich family filed in from someplace behind the altar and sat in their own pew up front. Mrs. Gingrich, Nathan, Mr. Gingrich, and four older people, Aaron's grandparents. All of them in dark clothes.

"Where's *Aardy?*" My stupid sister sounded loud even though she was whispering.

"Shhh." Mom whispered much more softly. "Maybe she's too upset. . . ."

I could understand that. I mean, Aardy had found Aaron's body. Maybe the doctor had put her on sedatives so she'd sleep for a month. What surprised me was to see that Nathan and Aaron's father had flown in from Minnesota. Right there he was, sitting down beside Nathan, on the other side from Mrs. Gingrich. He'd hardly ever bothered to come see his sons when they were both alive.

Then the minister came in, wearing black robes and stood behind the pulpit to start the service. The church got dead quiet.

"The Lord giveth, and the Lord taketh away. Blessed be the name of the Lord."

Didn't make any sense to me. I tuned out, staring at the back of Nathan's neck. His face when he came in hadn't showed me a thing except white and tight. I wondered whether he was getting any more sleep than I was. I knew from camping with him that he wasn't a real sound sleeper. . . .

He'd said he was napping when Aaron was killed? Since when did Nathan nap? He motored like a revved-up engine all the time.

Okay, maybe even Nathan napped once in a while. But . . . I didn't know what getting stabbed to death was like, but Aaron . . . Aaron must have made some noise. . . .

No. Damn it, no, this was no damn time to think about it. I tried to listen to the sermon, and I noticed the preacher was sweating. Even from the back of the church I could see his pink face shining. I guess it was a rough service. He said that all things happen in accordance with God's purpose, which sounded kind of lame. Same when he said Aaron was happy in heaven— I wondered if the Gingrich family was buying that any more than I was. Maybe they believed, but I knew Aaron shouldn't have died, damn it, especially not that way. God would comfort the Gingrich family? Lame. But when the preacher said we should all pray for justice, there was kind of a murmur in the church, and some deep-voiced man said, "Amen."

Was that what Aaron's family wanted? Was that what I wanted? Justice?

Not if it meant . . .

No. I wanted to stop thinking about it. Thinking wasn't going to bring Aaron back.

Mostly I just wanted it to be over.

The service ended, eventually. The family left the same way they'd come in. One of Aaron's grandparents sobbed, a raw, embarrassing noise that sounded very loud in the silence. Mrs. Gingrich hid her face in her

66

hands. Mr. Gingrich just looked fierce, even though there were tears on his cheeks. Nathan looked the same as when he came in.

Nobody said anything as we all filed out. I kept my head up. If anybody was giving me the evil eye, screw them. I was starting to get pissed off. Somebody had killed Aaron, and that person should pay, not me.

Out front, one of the gray-suited undertakers stopped us and asked whether we were going to the cemetery. Mom said, "No."

I said, "Mom, I want to."

She turned, and I was surprised to see how tired and wet-eyed she looked. "Jeremy, I don't think—"

"He was my best friend, Mom!"

Coach said, "I can take him, Mrs. Davis."

So I got to stand beside Coach and watch six members of the football team carry Aaron's casket out. I felt kind of grateful that I wasn't a pallbearer but mostly bummed that the Gingriches hadn't asked me. I should have been there for Aaron.

People piled into cars for the procession. It was a long, slow drive to the cemetery, winding between the hills in Coach's Jeep Cherokee with one of those little purple FUNERAL flags waving from the fender. Long, slow, and silent. Coach said something about football. I said, "I think I'm going to have to quit."

"Get out of this car." He was trying to joke, but I didn't say anything, so he said, "Jeremy, don't quit yet. Don't make any decision right now. Things will get better."

Yeah. Right.

Not anytime soon, that was for sure. I hate cemeteries. All the stupid heavy headstones, stupid flowers and trees, stupid sunshine when it should have been raining. I stood under the stupid tent beside Aaron's open grave, looking down into that raw hole in the clay and shale, and when I lifted my eyes, Mr. Gingrich scowled at me over his son's casket.

The minister said some more stuff. Ashes to ashes, dust to dust. Aaron's stepfather and mother dropped a little dirt on the casket. Nathan did, too. I faced him about five yards away, but he didn't look at me. His face still looked just the same, like a ceramic Nathan-mask.

"Go in peace," said the minister.

Nobody went. Nobody moved except Mr. Gingrich, striding over to me. He stopped in front of me and glared into my face from about six inches away. I think the only reason I didn't step back from him was because I was so damn tired of everything.

He whispered at me between his teeth, "Traitor."

"Mr. Gingrich, I'm sorry about Aaron," I said, meaning it.

"Judas! How dare you—"

"He was my best friend."

"Get out. Get away from him. Don't you ever—"

Coach said, "Mr. Gingrich, you're upset, you're saying things you'll regret—"

"You stay out of this!"

A policeman showed up at Mr. Gingrich's side. I knew him a little because he'd been keeping an eye on my house—it was getting so that I knew all the Pinto River cops. This one gave me a quiet, friendly look and touched Mr. Gingrich's elbow. "Your wife's waiting for you, sir."

Mr. Gingrich turned to him and stabbed his finger at me. "I want him out of here!"

"He has a right to be here, sir."

"It's time to go, anyway," Coach said.

Fine with me; I was tired. I followed him to his car, and we left.

More silence as he drove me home. Finally I said, "So you don't think I'm a liar?"

"I don't see any reason why you would lie, Jeremy. But there's a lot I don't understand."

"Me neither."

He pulled up in front of my house and said, "Oh, for God's sake." I saw too: yellow ick splattering the brick and the windows, along with sticky bits of shell. Somebody had egged the place while we were at Aaron's funeral.

chapter nine

When I finally got to sleep that night, I had a dream that was almost worse than lying awake. I don't remember all of it but I do remember that Aaron passed me the football and I fumbled and Coach yelled at me, "Liar! Liar!" but Aaron smiled and said it didn't matter, he was just being stupid, imagining things. Then somehow he had the football again and he ran it between the other players, only they weren't players, they were couples in tuxedos and evening gowns, he was running through the prom and every footstep left a blood trail. I screamed, "Aaron, *run!*" and he ran like a devil was after him, over the roof of the church and down Main Street and through Rose's café and his dad's store and all over Pinto River, leaving a blood trail everywhere. He ran into the development, down through my basement and up again and across his lawn, where all the dead flowers were lying, and instead of a football he was carrying his severed head under his arm, tracking blood like floods of red ink out of a lie detector machine. I screamed,

"The river! Head for the river!" like in an old movie, like the bloodhounds were after him. We ran and ran, I ran with him up mountains and over cliffs and down the winding river road, and he left blood on the sky and blood on the boulders and scrub pines and blood on the asphalt as he ran. When we got to the river and he dived in, the water turned blood red. He dived into the swimming hole and disappeared, he didn't come up again, and I knew he was dying but I couldn't do a thing to help him, I stood there dripping sweat and tears, with my legs aching like my heart, just stood there in the shallows with a giant crayfish clamped onto my ankles like shackles. Only Aaron's head stayed on the surface. It floated past me, looked at me and said, "Booger, I'm scared—"

I woke up sweating. My throat hurt like I had a knife blade stuck in it. I heard someone whimpering and sobbing, and it wasn't me; it came from across the hallway. My stupid sister, crying in her sleep. Then she sighed and quieted down. Maybe she woke up. Outside, a car blasted past with the stereo thumping. Somebody yelled almost as loud as the stereo, and I heard a rock or something hit the front of the house.

God damn everything. I lunged out of bed and stomped downstairs. Without turning the light on, I plugged the phone in and quick-dialed my father.

On the third ring he picked up. "Yo."

"Hey, you're there."

"I ought to be," he said. "It's three in the morning."

There were a lot of things I could have said, like he could have still been hanging out at the Tipple Tavern, or he could have been with his girlfriend, or if he wanted me not to call at three in the morning, he should have called me back when he got my message. But all I said was, "Yeah, and people are throwing rocks at the house."

"Just the usual dumb crap. Have they hosed down the car and dumped flour on it yet?"

"No, because it's in the garage!"

"They could get in there if they wanted to. Break a window, slash your mom's tires—"

"Yeah, and they might try it."

"So what do you want me to do about it, son?"

"You're the security expert." Like I said before, my father works security at the county courthouse. It must have been because he knew somebody, since he was never any kind of cop. When criminal court is in session, he mans the metal detector at the front door and he gets to help guard prisoners. Between that and hanging out at the Tipple, he knows everything. Even though I hadn't heard a word from him, I could count on it that he knew what I meant about people throwing rocks.

I told him, "They egged the place yesterday."

"So? Just the usual stupidity, like I said. Did it wash off?"

"Mom said don't bother, just leave it that way for a while. Like we don't care."

"Your mother is a wise woman," Dad said.

"Whatever," I said. Dad always said Mom was a wise woman, but that hadn't kept him from walking out on her. I told him, "I need a gun for self-defense."

He sighed.

"Dad?"

"Is your mother asleep?"

"I guess so." She wasn't asking me what the heck I was doing on the phone at three A.M.

"Okay. Don't wake her. I'm coming over."

The guys with the cranked-up sound system went past twice more before Dad got there. I kept the lights off and got a look at them out the window. Some kind of dark-colored pickup truck, with Baja lights and a roll bar. Each time they roared past, they yelled and threw something.

Finally Dad tapped at the door. He never came inside the house, so I went outside to talk with him. "Watch where you step," he said, shining a big security-dude flashlight on a paper bag that had splatted open against the doorstep. "Looks like nice fresh cow manure."

It smelled like nice fresh cow manure, too. I just stood there shivering. Except for streetlights and his flashlight and some people's landscape lights and stuff, it was dark out there. I didn't like it.

"You scared?" Dad asked.

"Yes!" I had got to a point where I didn't even mind being a coward.

"That's dumb. You don't have to be scared of those jerks."

"Like hell," I said.

"Son, this is all going to blow over. And these cretins aren't going to do jack except yell and throw crap."

Mostly for the sake of argument I said, "Yeah, but what about the murderer?"

"What about him?"

"He's still out there!" And all of a sudden I realized it could be true. There really could be a murderer hiding in the black pines and hemlocks that grew like a beard all over the mountains. Or maybe closer. Maybe behind a boulder in the river bottom. Maybe watching from the poplars at the edge of my yard. Damn dark shaggy trees everywhere, damn rocks and caves, damn abandoned mines and foggy hills, he could be anywhere.

Dad looked at me kind of odd.

"The psycho who killed Aaron!" I said, getting louder. "Or intruder, whatever, maybe he's a serial killer, maybe he likes to carve up high school jocks."

Dad started to laugh.

"Stop it!" I hated him. "I need a gun, Dad!"

"Get a clue, son!"

That hurt. I yelled, "What the hell are you talking about?"

"Shush! You'll wake your mother." He kind of gulped, then mostly stopped laughing. "You know who killed Aaron as well as the cops do."

"I don't know anything!"

"C'mere." He took me by the elbow and headed me toward his old Hyundai. Once I sat in the passenger seat and locked the door I felt calmer. Also, Dad was being serious now, which helped.

He settled himself behind the wheel but he didn't start the car. He said, "I shouldn't have laughed. All you know is what's been in the news, right?"

I gave him a look and didn't answer.

"Right," he said. "But there's a lot they don't tell you. Such as, there is no evidence at all that any intruder was ever in that house."

"Maybe he wore gloves," I said.

"That only accounts for fingerprints. What about hairs, fibers, footprints, saliva, maybe a spot or two of blood? You can't go someplace without leaving evidence. Dirt, dead skin particles, whatever—with the technology the state police have got, they would have found something if an intruder had been there. And there was no sign of forcible entry. How—"

"Maybe some door wasn't locked."

"The front door was unlocked when Cecily got home. Nathan said he locked the doors. Then he changed his story and said he wasn't sure. His first story, he said he locked the doors and went to bed, his sister woke him up screaming, he went down and saw Aaron's body, he called 911. He didn't say a word about your phone calls. But the cops have your voice on the answering machine, they have Jamy and Cecily and two others to verify that you made the calls, so Nathan changed his story. Now he says it's the phone that woke him up, and he answered it before Cecily came home and he saw the body. But to get to the downstairs phone from his bedroom, he had to walk past the body. So he says he got it upstairs. But that phone is in his parents' bedroom, and the carpet had just been vacuumed, and there are no footmarks. And the downstairs phone has bloodstains on it."

I started to feel cold, remembering how I had felt so relieved when Nathan had answered, and now Dad was saying he had picked up the phone with—with blood on his hands.

"Maybe it got there when he called 911."

"Okay, maybe. He says he wasn't thinking, he touched Aaron, and that's when he got blood all over him. Okay, fine, but Cecily would know whether he had blood on him when she got home, right?"

Oh, my God.

I just sat there. Couldn't make myself ask.

"And she's not saying," Dad answered the question I couldn't ask. "The cops try to talk with her or hook her up to the polygraph, she just gets hysterical."

God have mercy. Poor Aardy.

"They can't make her testify against her brother anyway," Dad said, "but they don't need to. There's plenty of physical evidence. For starters, Nathan's footprints are in the blood trail all over the house."

Cold. I felt cold. So cold I couldn't speak.

"Somebody—and I for one think it must have been Nathan—had cleaned up the blood trail," Dad said, "but you can still see it under black light. Kitchen, living room, stairs, kitchen again, and Nathan's footprints are in it all the way."

I found my voice. "So he was stupid, he cleaned it up, his footprints got in it—"

"But there are no other footprints in it. Only his and Aaron's."

I turned away, staring out the car window at the night like it could tell me something.

I heard Dad's voice. "Use your brain, son."

God damn everything. I whispered, "But . . . but why would Nathan kill Aaron?"

"Ah." Dad actually sounded like I'd said something right. "That's the prosecution's one weak point. Motive. But with all the physical evidence, they don't really need to prove motive. I mean, brother killing brother, ask the cops. Something like ninety percent of domestic calls where it's brother fighting brother, sooner or later it ends up in murder. But I bet the funeral preacher didn't mention the first crime in the Bible, did he? I bet he didn't talk about Cain and Abel."

I didn't say anything, just sat there, but Dad kept

talking. "They'll send him up for psychiatric examination," he said. "He'll probably plead insane. Maybe he *is* psycho. You should have heard the cops at the bar talking about his lie detector test."

That made me sit up and listen. "What about his lie detector test?"

"No reactions. None. No nerves, no emotions, nothing. Like he's got no conscience at all."

Cold. So cold. Trying to joke, I said, "Me, I flunked the baseline."

"Oh, that old thing where they tell you to choose a number between one and five?"

Why did he always have to know everything? I clenched my teeth. "I can't believe Nathan did it."

"Son, like I said, get a clue. The minute I heard about the autopsy, I knew it was the brother."

"Huh? How?"

"Seventy-three stab wounds, for God's sake, that's how! That's not from some burglar the kid walked in on, or even a serial killer. Seventy-three stab wounds, that's rage that's been building for years, that's a personal grudge, that's hatred. Nobody hates that bad except family."

I hated him. "That doesn't make sense."

"Yes, it does. Ask any cop what calls are the most dangerous, and they'll tell you: domestic. Most murders, who do you suspect first? The family."

My head hurt from listening to him, my throat

hurt, and my eyes hurt, and my chest hurt. I had to make my voice hard to talk at all. "I still want a gun." I needed one. Hate calls. People throwing rocks in the night. Mr. Gingrich.

"Forget it, son. Even if it was legal, I wouldn't get you one."

"But I'm scared!"

"Worst reason. Worst thing you can do when your emotions are out of control is grab a gun." Dad's voice changed gears into low. "I almost killed your mother once that way. Did she ever tell you?"

I sat there with my mouth open.

"She didn't tell you? Your mother is too kind. Yes, I grabbed the pistol, and if it had been loaded, I would have offed her." Now he sounded like he was talking about a TV show or something. "I could have been in jail now, instead of sitting here baby-sitting you."

Baby-sitting?

"Too bad Nathan didn't have a gun," Dad said. "Bullets don't make nearly so much mess."

I burst out, "Nathan didn't do it! He couldn't have! Why would he?"

"Get real, son. There could be a thousand reasons. Aaron's rather crude sense of humor, for one."

"But Aaron never meant—"

"Doesn't matter. You know how they fought. Didn't Aaron break Nathan's arm one time?"

"Yeah, but he didn't mean to. He was bigger—"

"And he knew it. Gave Nathan reason to hate him. So. Take sibling rivalry, maybe add a girl—"

"There wasn't a girl! Not that I know of."

"But you don't know everything, obviously." God, I hate it when Dad gets sarcastic. "Anyway, Nathan did it. You know it and I know it and the police know it."

I demanded, "If everybody's so damn sure it was Nathan, why don't they arrest him?"

"They did," Dad said. "A few hours ago."

chapter ten

"What a way to start senior year," I said to Rose as I helped her put together a six-foot sub for somebody's Sunday afternoon football party. "Most people, the worst that happens in their senior year is that somebody gets in a car accident."

"Car accident might happen yet," Rose said. "It's only October. They asked for provolone cheese."

I got out the cheese rounds and started laying them the length of the sub.

"Wait till spring for car accidents," Rose said, laying on the spicy Italian salami. "Prom time."

"Jeez, I hope not." Things were rough enough. I'd pretty much blown the first month of school, felt so bad a lot of days I didn't go, couldn't concentrate when I did, and I was still catching up, and the football team was lousy and like I'd told Coach, I wasn't playing, and . . . I don't know, life just sucked.

"How's it going?" Rose asked like she was a mind reader.

"Okay, I guess."

"You guess?"

I grunted and reached for the onions. Threw on enough to make somebody cry. Yeah, things were going better, like, the cops had caught the guys who were throwing rocks and stuff at the house. And Mrs. Ledbetter a.k.a. Pinto River Info Central had found out who was making hate calls. The CIA could take lessons from Mrs. Ledbetter. Anyway, Mrs. Ledbetter had talked with the minister, and he had talked with certain people, and most of the threats had stopped.

And school wasn't so bad anymore. A few kids called me names, but most of them acted the same as before. People were calmer, and starting to talk about football and stuff, not just Aaron's murder. They were still taking sides, but now that Nathan was officially charged with murder, some people had changed their minds. Pinto River wasn't worried about a serial killer anymore. Instead, some people were afraid of Nathan, because he wasn't in jail; he was at home with electronic bracelets on his ankles. Yeah, the Gingriches were back in their house, with fresh paint and new carpeting, and Nathan was there with them.

But Aardy wasn't. Mrs. Ledbetter, who knew all, said little Cecily was so upset, nearly out of her mind, that her parents had sent her to stay at some kind of home or something in Wisconsin or someplace, to get her away from Pinto River.

But some people said the Gingriches had sent her away to keep the police from finding out what she knew.

And the people who were afraid of Nathan said Aardy's parents had sent her away because they were afraid Nathan might kill her too.

I tried not to think about it. Anyway, I wasn't afraid of Nathan, and I didn't feel like I needed a gun anymore. Hell, I could knock Nathan down with one hand tied behind me.

It had been over a month now. CNN and *USA Today* had showed up after Nathan was arrested, wanting to interview me, but I wasn't giving interviews, and they were long gone. Life was pretty much back to normal. Dad had actually called me a couple of times, now that I didn't feel like talking to him. The worst was over, right?

So why didn't I feel better?

"Jeremy," Rose said, "for crying out loud, that's way too many onions. Spread them out. Here, I'll do it." Out front, the bell dinged as somebody came in. A customer for me to take care of. Rose had me on the counter all the time now because I was nice and polite. It was just my luck to be so polite.

It was an old couple. Well, not real old. Kind of medium old. Still walking around. I thought they looked at me odd while I took their order for spaghetti and meatballs, but I could have been imagining it. I told them it would be ten minutes, and I was handing the old guy his change when the wife asked me straight out, "Aren't you the boy who said Nathan done it?"

That took me by surprise because nobody had ever said it to my face before. I just stood there staring.

"He never said Nathan done it, Ruth," the old guy snapped at her. "He said Aaron was afraid of Nathan. There's a difference."

"Um, right," I managed to say.

"Well, it just goes to show," the woman told me kindly, "nobody should never say nothing against family to an outsider. Because it might get around, and now look what happened? They think that boy done it."

"Um, yes, ma'am."

All through lunch rush, I kept thinking about the way they'd recognized me. How'd they know me? I hadn't been on TV or in the newspaper or anything, but damn near everybody knew who I was. It made me think of three, maybe four years ago, when a senior class girl got raped. They caught the rapist, some guy from the trailer park, I don't remember who he was. I remembered who she was, though. Everybody did. She had a name, but nobody used it. She was just "the girl who got raped." Like, it wasn't her fault, but for the rest of her life in Pinto River that was what she was gonna be, the girl who got raped.

And what was I going to be? The boy who was with Aaron before it happened? The boy who pointed the finger? The boy who said Nathan did it?

It was never going to be over.

I wondered whether the Gingriches were trying to make it be over. Whether they had done anything to Aaron's room when they got the new carpet to replace the one with bloodstains on it and holes cut in it by the cops. I wondered whether they had painted Aaron's room when they had painted over the rusty splatters on the walls. I wondered whether they had put his things away.

There was no way of knowing. I wasn't welcome in that house anymore.

I wondered, if the cops came in there with their black light machine now, could they still find the blood trail?

It didn't matter. The blood trail was still around. Staining my life. And it was never going to wash away.

Rose sent me home mid-afternoon. I was dead tired and I smelled like onions. But instead of going inside I just stood in the garage doorway looking at my bike and remembering the last time I rode it—and just then the Gingrich family drove by, Mr. and Mrs. in the front seat and Nathan in the back. All three of them turned their heads and gave me the stare, cold as fish.

I went a little crazy.

I didn't even swear. I just slammed into the house, and right there on the counter sat the pumpkin Mom had bought because Jamy still likes to carve one for Halloween. It was a monster pumpkin, so big Mom had made me lug it in from the car, and it didn't have eyes yet but it was looking at me, giving me the blank stare.

No goddamn pumpkin better look at me that way. I grabbed the biggest butcher knife out of the drawer and went for it. I stabbed it so hard, I whammed the knife into the rind up to the hilt. One. I yanked the knife out and stabbed again. Two. And again, three, and again, four, and again, five, six, seven . . . I slashed, I chopped, I was starting to pant, and pumpkin shell and pumpkin juice flew all over the kitchen floor.

"Booger," screamed Jamy's voice behind me, "what the—"

"Go away," I panted, stabbing. Ten, eleven, twelve. What the hell was the brat doing home, anyway? Why wasn't she at the game or something? Or out shopping with Mom?

She yelled, "That's my pumpkin!"

"Go *away*!"

"What are you *doing*?"

I turned on her with the knife in my hand. "PRACTICING!"

My eyes must have looked cold-out crazy. Her face went white. She backed away.

I drove the knife into the pumpkin again. Stab, stab, stab, fifteen, sixteen, seventeen. My chest burned for air, my arms ached, my hands hurt, I sweated and started to feel weak. I'd stabbed a messy hole in the pumpkin but I had to keep going. Around twenty-seven I lost count. A little while after that, I quit. I think I'd got to maybe thirty-three, tops.

I dropped the butcher knife in the pumpkin slop on the counter and stood there just staring at what I'd done, breathing hard and swallowing again and again and starting to shiver as my sweat went cold. What would it take to stab something—somebody—seventy-three times?

I'd never tried to imagine something so evil.

God have mercy.

"Yaaaah!" shrilled a karate screech right behind me.

God damn, I jumped! I turned, and there stood Jamy with a bloodred knife in her hand. "Yaaaah!" she yelled again as she lunged at me.

She scared me so bad, I almost peed my pants. "Jamy, no!" I yelled—screamed, really. My hands flew up. Her knife skittered past them and whammed against my chest, leaving a red smear on my T-shirt. I was bleeding! That's how I felt, even though I was starting to realize it wasn't a knife, really. It was a rubber bayonet I used to play war with when I was a kid, and she'd smeared gobs of red lipstick all over it.

"I'm killing you!" she screamed, stabbing again. Okay, it was just a rubber knife, and you'd think I could have fended her off. I'm a football jock, for God's sake, or at least I used to be, and Jamy's younger and smaller and I should have been able to stop her with one hand. But she attacked me like she meant it with all the hate in the universe, and it seemed so real, it just stunned me stupid. I couldn't react. All I did was back away with my hands up, and she stabbed them out of the way and got me in the shoulder.

"Stop it, Jamy!" I yelled.

"Make me!" She came at me fierce as a fox and stabbed me with her rubber knife in the belly.

"Stop, damn it!" I stumbled back from her.

"Make me stop, Butthead! Yaaaaah!"

I grabbed her by the arms and tried to hold her still. She fought worse than a wildcat, and I was scared to hold her too hard, because I might hurt her. She sliced at my forearms and squirmed away from me and stabbed me in the gut again.

"Grab your big damn stupid knife!" she yelled.

What the hell? The butcher knife, lying there on the counter? I couldn't do that—I might hurt her! That butcher knife was as scary as a poisonous snake to me. I backed away, begging, "Jamy, stop, please!"

"No. I'm going to kill you and you can't stop me." She lunged at me again.

I am going to kill you. It made me sweat ice.

And you can't stop me.

I couldn't. Not without hurting her.

I backed away from her, yelling and begging, but I couldn't get the knife away from her, couldn't knock her down, couldn't even hit her. I slipped in orange pumpkin blood and fell on the floor and I just lay there. If it had been somebody else attacking me, a stranger or some jerk from school, I would have been able to defend myself better, but it was Jamy. Jamy, my sister. God have mercy, I couldn't have hurt her to save my life.

chapter eleven

Somebody pounded on the door.

Jamy stood over me panting for a moment, then she said, "Now what?" and she sounded normal again, bratty, like somebody was interrupting her TV show. She dropped her bloody rubber bayonet on top of me, ran to the door, and stretched on tiptoe to look out the peephole. "Oh, God," she said, "it's the cops."

I sighed and closed my eyes, feeling dead.

"What do I do?" Jamy bleated. I opened my eyes and looked at her. She was just standing by the door with her arms crossed, with one of her sneaker toes on top of the other. It felt weird looking at her from the floor, and what the hell was she scared of?

I said, "Let them in."

"I can't!"

I sighed again, harder, heaved myself to my feet, walked out there, and opened the door. I wasn't afraid, because I didn't feel like anything was real anymore. It was like I was walking through cobwebs, like a bad dream. Come to think of it, most of my life had felt that way lately.

Two cops stood on the doorstep, and I knew both of them. Their eyes widened when they saw me.

"It's just lipstick," Jamy blurted.

One of the officers asked, "What's going on here?"

I said, "I was stabbing a pumpkin."

They just stared at me. The other cop asked, "Were you screaming? One of the neighbors heard screaming."

I shook my head—not to say I wasn't screaming, which would have been a lie, but because I didn't like what I was thinking. I asked, "Why didn't somebody call you guys when Aaron screamed? He must have screamed." Even to me I sounded dumb as a plum, but at least I'd said it.

"Been wondering about that myself, son."

Silence.

"People don't like to get involved," the second cop said.

"But he must have screamed more than I did."

The cops looked at each other. Then, "You were stabbing a pumpkin?" one cop prompted like he was coaxing a crazy person.

I said, "I wanted to see how many times I could stab it before I pooped out."

"How many did you get to?" asked both cops at once.

But I was looking at the red smears Jamy had put all over my arms and chest. "Sixteen, seventeen," I said, counting the marks, but the cops took that as my answer.

"I got mad at him," Jamy explained, "and I put lipstick on a rubber knife—"

Twenty, twenty-one. "She stabbed me twenty-one times," I told the cops.

They looked at each other and rolled their eyes. "Look," one of them said, "next time you kids play murder, warn the neighbors first, okay?" They started to turn away.

"Hey," Jamy said, "you would know—is it true . . ."

They stood there, polite, waiting to hear her question.

"A girl in school, her uncle is the ambulance driver," Jamy said, "and she says he said Aaron's eyes were gouged out. Is that true?"

I ran. If they answered, I never heard. I ran for the bathroom, and by the time I got there, I was crying so hard I couldn't see.

Half an hour later, I was in the shower when I heard Mom yelling, "Jeremy? Jeremy!" and knocking hard on the bathroom door.

God damn, she was going to yell at me to stop wasting water, I'd been in the shower for twenty minutes.

God, when was life going to give me a break? I hollered above the water noise, "*What!*"

She yelled, "Are you okay?"

"Huh?" *Huh, hell, pay attention.* I'd heard her, but I didn't know what to say.

"*Are you okay?*"

I sighed and turned the water off. By then I was mostly done bawling, and I hoped the shower noise had kept anybody from hearing. I had scrubbed the lipstick marks off my arms. At least the brat hadn't gone for my neck or my face. Probably afraid she'd put a rubber bayonet in my eye. Aaron's eyes gouged out . . . the thought still made me sick to my stomach. Was I okay? Compared to what? Compared to any day this past month, yeah, I was fine. I grumped, "Why wouldn't I be okay?"

"Jamy's afraid she might have upset you."

"Tell Jamy to go milk herself!"

"Jeremy," Mom reproached me, "she's crying. What in the world is going on? I can't get any sense out of her."

I stood there listening to the water dripping off me like rain.

"Jeremy?"

"Just a minute. I'll be out."

I took my time drying off and getting dressed. Needed time to calm down, think, figure things out. Finally I pulled on jeans and a T-shirt and barefooted downstairs. My sister was sitting at the kitchen table, not crying anymore but not helping, either, while Mom stowed groceries in the cupboards.

I walked up behind the brat, leaned over, and hugged her around the shoulders.

It's not like I do that all the time. Hardly ever, I guess. She stiffened at first like she was surprised, but then she turned in her chair and hugged back.

I let go of her and mussed her hair. "So, you got a clue?" I asked.

"Huh?"

"You got it through your head? I would never take a knife to you."

She kind of gulped, and I knew I'd guessed right. I sat down across from her.

"You've been scared ever since Aaron got killed," I said.

She nodded, then whispered, "They . . . they sent Aardy away . . ." Damn, she was crying again. Tears on her face.

"You think that's why? Because big brothers kill their little sisters all the time?"

"I don't *know*. I—never got—to talk with her. . . ."

All of a sudden I saw—jeez, I'd been so sorry for myself since Aaron died, I'd never thought. . . . I blurted, "You miss Aardy?"

"Of course I miss her, bung brain! Duh!"

I just sat there, feeling toad stupid.

"And I feel bad for her."

I recognized the quiver in Jamy's voice. But there was nothing I could say, because there wasn't a thing she could do to help Aardy. Any more than I could help Aaron.

Feeling like I had to do *something,* I looked for the pumpkin mess, but somebody had already cleaned it up. "Mom," I called, "I'll get Jamy another pumpkin."

Mom just nodded, staying out of it.

"You better," Jamy said, her voice stronger now. "So what about you? You got a clue now?"

"Huh?"

"You got it through your head?" She mimicked my voice. "Nathan killed Aaron."

I didn't say anything. I just sat there, trying to visualize it like visualizing a football play beforehand, trying to—trying to understand, damn it. But I still couldn't quite get a grip, trying to take in the idea of Aaron, stabbed seventy-three times, head almost severed, eyes gouged out—God. Thinking about it made my whole gut go sick and watery.

My mind winced away one more time, telling me it couldn't have been Nathan. Telling me that Nathan was a skinny debate club nerd and Aaron was bigger, stronger, so why hadn't he defended himself?

But it was no good. I knew the answer to that one now. Aaron hadn't defended himself because he was attacked by somebody he just couldn't hurt, that was why.

And I knew too well who that had to be. Anybody else, and Aaron would have taken them apart—

But it was up to the judge and the jury, not to me.

Or like the minister had said at the funeral, up to a higher authority. And yeah, I did want justice.

Finally I said, "If Nathan really did do it, I hope he fries in hell."

Mom closed a cupboard door with a slam and said, her voice as flat as plywood, "I imagine he's already there."

chapter twelve

With the springtime sun warm on my shoulders, I sat in the bleachers, Mom on one side of me and Jamy on the other, all of us dressed up like for another funeral. About ninety percent of Pinto River was there at the football stadium, and a swarm of newspeople, photographers, TV crews, CNN, the networks, the whole hairy enchilada. And cops—township police, state police, rent-a-cops, security out the wazoo. And just like at Aaron's funeral, there were all these people and I never heard a crowd so quiet. You could hear the robins singing in the bushes beyond the stadium fence, it was so quiet.

Morgan and her family filed in below us. I didn't call to her, but I waved, and she saw me and waved back.

My nosy sister asked, "Who you waving at?" and glanced up. "Oh," she said, and she went back to looking at all the pictures of Aaron in the program booklet. Aaron as a football player, Aaron as a little kid, Aaron horsing around with Aardy. And Nathan. Lots of pictures of Aaron with Nathan. The Gingriches had probably made sure of that. They had hired a platoon of lawyers—they were spending their life savings, Mrs. Ledbetter said. She'd heard they'd double-mortgaged the house. Anyway, the lawyers were doing all kinds of legal back flips to delay Nathan's trial, and meanwhile the Gingriches were doing everything they could to make Nathan look like a loving brother. Including the new scoreboard, which Nathan was going to dedicate to Aaron's memory, which was why we were all here today.

I didn't want to look at the pictures of Aaron right now. Later. I kind of hoped Morgan would come sit with me. She'd been my date for the prom, and we'd had a good time, and thank God, nobody had gotten killed in a car wreck, although one boy had rolled his girlfriend's old pink Tracker and put himself and her in the hospital. They were supposed to be out for graduation in a few weeks.

Dad was coming to graduation. He'd promised. And Mom had promised she would be polite to him. He could sit with her and Jamy.

I looked for Morgan again and saw that she wasn't going to sit with me today. She had turned away to sit with her family. Okay. In a weird way, today felt like baccalaureate or something. Mom must have been thinking about graduation too, because she said, "I'm glad I'm not on the school board."

"They decide yet?"

"Not yet." They had to rule whether Nathan was allowed to attend graduation. The criminal court judge had said yeah, okay, innocent until proved guilty and all that, Nathan could go anyplace in Pinto River as long as he wore his electronic ankle bracelets and had a parent supervising him at all times. The Gingriches wanted Nathan to graduate with his class. So now it was up to the school board. Nathan had been on home instruction all year, and he'd made passing grades. I wondered what it was like to be a teacher and go to Nathan's house to see whether he did his calculus homework. I wondered whether he was applying to colleges. If he was, I wondered what he told them about himself.

I still wondered whether it was possible that he hadn't done it. Whether it was possible, as Mr. and Mrs. Gingrich kept insisting, that the real murderer was out there somewhere.

"There they are," Mom said as Mr. and Mrs. Gingrich and Nathan walked onto the football field with a dozen TV cameras swiveling to film them.

From up in the bleachers, Nathan looked very small to me, like a plastic doll or something. Aaron had never looked so small on a football field. Aaron would have been laughing if he could have seen it, a draped platform perched on the fifty-yard line and all the VIPs sitting on it and a bazillion potted flowers all around. He would have wanted to run broken field patterns between all those flowerpots.

Watching the Gingriches walk up the steps to the platform, Mom murmured, "I can't imagine what they're going through. How they go on. I just can't."

We all watched them take their seats in front of the high school principal and the school board and the mayor and the minister. Mr. Gingrich, Mrs. Gingrich, Nathan in the middle, with the whole crowd as quiet as my breathing.

Mom said, "I feel for them. I wonder what they really think, in their heart of hearts, about Nathan."

She had spoken softly, but an older man in front of us turned around and said, "They have to believe he's innocent. They just have to. What else are they supposed to think?"

"I know," Mom said.

"It's bad enough they lost their one son the way they did. They can't let themselves lose both of their boys."

Mom nodded. She hadn't meant to get into a conversation with a stranger.

"And that Nathan boy looks like a nice clean-cut kid," said the man in a low voice. "Why would he have done such a thing? That's what I can't get past. Why?"

"We don't know."

"But wouldn't you think, if there was something really wrong with him, the parents would have noticed?"

The woman who was sitting next to the man turned around, too. "You got to wonder what went on in that house," she whispered. "I just don't get it."

Mom shook her head.

"Maybe it was one of those Dr. Jekyll and Mr. Hyde things," the man said. "Split personality."

Mom said again, "We don't know."

I wouldn't have thought the brat was even listening, but she looked up from her program book and said, "Maybe Aaron had something Nathan didn't have."

"Such as?" I said just to argue with her.

"Friends." She lifted the program book and pointed at one of the pictures. "Jeremy, shouldn't you be there?"

I looked. It was a good picture of Aaron after a football game, in his dirty uniform, grinning, with his arm around another player's shoulders. The other player was cut off, along with part of Aaron's arm. Yeah, the cut-off player would have been me. I recognized the picture; the Gingriches had given me a copy at the time. Now they wanted me out of Aaron's picture and out of their lives.

"Huh," I said.

"Shouldn't that be you?" The brat was insisting on an answer.

"Jamy, shush," Mom said. "They're about to start."

All of a sudden I couldn't stand it. I stood up. "Mom, I've gotta get out of here. I'll walk home."

She gawked up at me. "Jeremy, what—"

The old guy in front of us exclaimed, "Aren't you the boy who ratted on him?"

He said it like I was a celebrity or something, but I felt like he'd stabbed me in the gut. There it was again, the blood trail, all over me, all over the whole damn town, and it would never totally go away, and I . . . my fists clenched, but there was not a freaking thing I could do about it. I turned away and blundered out of the bleachers, pushing past people's knees and stepping on their feet. I loped down the stadium steps two at a time. Some reporter spotted me and called, "Jeremy! Jeremy Davis!" but I kept going. When I got out of the stadium gates, I ran.

I ran like my life depended on it. Some news van chased me for a while, but I cut through somebody's woods to the river road and lost them. Kept running, but not running home. Didn't know where I was going. Not to Aaron's grave; I'd been there, and it didn't help. No, I just wanted to run, run, out of Pinto River and out of the dark shaggy scowling mountains and off the edge of the universe if possible. I felt like I could have run that far and I wanted to, even with my suit flapping and my dress-up shoes blistering my heels. Run, run, fists pumping, heart drumming, I must have run five miles along the river road. Coach would have been proud of me. Run, run, pulse thumping in my head, river air rushing in my lungs felt mint crisp. I wasn't thinking of Nathan or Aaron, wasn't thinking of any-thing. But something made me swerve off the road, slow down, walk down the rocky trail, and there I was at the swimming hole.

He had smiled. Never mind, I'm being stupid, he had said, imagining things. Time to get home.

I would never understand what had happened.

In my sweated-up suit I sat on the same boulder where I'd sat that day. Sun warm on my shoulders. My breathing quieted. Sunbeams made the shallow water golden. I stared. I didn't see any crayfish, but I saw tadpoles swarming like starlings, and off to one side, some minnows flashing.

I ought to go fishing this summer. Hadn't been for years. Aaron and Nathan and I used to go fishing for sunnies when we were kids—

God, I hurt.

I must have sat there a long time. After a while I realized I was still carrying the program book in my clenched hand. I opened it and looked at the crumpled pictures of Aaron and Nathan. How could Nathan have done that to Aaron? To me? To all of us?

Hindsight might be a liar, like the detective said, but still. . . . There should have been something I could have done or said, something somebody could have done to make things . . . different.

I looked into the river some more. In my nightmare it had turned to blood, but it would never really do that. It just kept on flowing. A kingfisher flew upriver in a blur of neon blue, made a noise like a ratchet, and snagged a minnow out of the shallows with its bayonet beak. It all happened so fast that if I'd blinked, I would have missed it.

The angle of the sun had changed, and in my sweaty clothes I was starting to get cold.

I still sat there. Didn't want to go home.

I'm afraid to go home, he had said.

Footsteps scrunched on the shale and gravel of the trail.

I looked up, and for a freaky second I expected it to be Aaron, his hair shining reddish in the sun, like maybe he'd been out on his bike or out running and I was in my blue jeans instead of in my good suit with sweat and dirt all over it, and Aaron was meeting me at the swimming hole, saying "Hey, Booger, what's up, man?"

Actually, it was my mom and my sister. Jamy yelled, "Booger! See, Mom, I told you!"

"May we join you?" Still in her heels and dress, Mom perched on the other boulder.

"You're going to get your skirt dirty," I told her.

"So what is this, role reversal?"

Damn, she made me smile. "How was it?" I asked.

"Lots of speeches that didn't say anything."

"Awful," Jamy summarized, sitting on my rock beside me. "Hey, tadpoles!"

We all looked at the tadpoles like we'd never seen any before.

I said to the river, "I'm never going to understand."

Jamy said, "I wish he'd just confess and go to jail. Then maybe Aardy could come home."

Mom shook her head like it would never happen. "That poor girl—if she saw him with blood on his clothes, on his hands. . . ."

Aardy was never going to be the same.

Neither was I.

"Even if he did confess, I still wouldn't get it," I said. "Or even if they find him guilty . . . I just don't damn understand. How. Why. I mean, I knew him and Aaron practically my whole life."

"That's what I keep thinking," Mom said quietly. "How you can know somebody for years, and just not know them at all." The way her eyes darkened, I knew she was thinking about Dad. She had thought she knew him, and he had turned out to be a different person.

"I don't have any answer for you, honey," Mom said. "I'm sorry."

"But that's kind of an answer," I said. I mean, she was there. My brat sister was there. Two out of three ain't bad. And the blood trail . . . the blood trail ended at Pinto River.

We all sat looking at the river like we'd never seen running water before. Sunlight on the ripples. Tadpoles. A butterfly the color of Aaron's hair landed on the moist gravel at the edge and posed there a second, fanning its wings, before it lifted off again. The way it flew, it was like swimming in the sunlight.

"Pretty," Jamy said.

I let out some sort of grunt or snort or something. Mom looked at me. "What was that about?"'

I couldn't have explained in a million years. I just stood up. "Come on. I'm hungry."

Time to go home.

DATE DUE

FEB 1 4 85					